The Hoopster

by Alan Lawrence Sitomer

SCHOLASTIC INC.

New York Toronto London Auckland Sydney
Mexico City New Delhi Hong Kong Buenos Aires

Copyright © 2005 by Alan Lawrence Sitomer.

All rights reserved.
Published by Scholastic Inc.,
557 Broadway, New York, NY 10012,
by arrangement with Hyperion Books for Children
Printed in the U.S.A.

ISBN-13: 978-0-545-19643-7
ISBN-10: 0-545-19643-4

SCHOLASTIC and associated logos and designs are trademarks
and/or registered trademarks of Scholastic Inc.

1 2 3 4 5 6 7 8 9 10   40   18 17 16 15 14 13 12 11 10 09

Dedicated to my grandfathers:
each of them special,
each of them influential,
each of them loved.

And a special thanks to my Awesome Wife;
Clipper-Lovin' Brother; Mom (a tissue please);
Taaron (zee amazing one); Andrea (and her kitchen);
E.R., for always supporting (and B.K. too);
R.V. (mon frère kindred); Junior in S.F.;
Larr-Dogg in WA; my Grams; Brittney B.;
& G-Money, my mainest of main men (what up, Chuck?).

Plus, a major SHOUT-OUT is due to the magnificent
book pros in my corner. Truly, I'm blessed with a Dream Team.
Thanks, Wendy, for your perpetual awesomeness; Christopher,
for your keen red pen; Angus, for your unfailing optimism;
Al Z, for being the most consummately incredible agent with
which a writer could ever hope to work
(Wow, am I forever grateful to you!); and Jerry the K,
for your passion, vision, and tenacity.

Hey, Dad, check it out.

I

A hard beat pumped from a radio by the fence. Ten players, twenty sneakers, two rims, one basketball: that's all there was. That's all they needed.

A ball sailed through the air. *SWISH!*

Across the court, a player tried to dribble past a defender and take him to the hole, but the pick was weak and the defense clogged the middle. A shot was forced up off balance. Two players battled for position under the boards. Shawn, a white player for the Skins, got the tip, dribbled back up-court away from the basket, then stopped, popped, and nailed a three-point basket.

"*Unh*—bay-beee!" he boasted to no one in particular. With his arm raised and a smile on his face, Shawn trotted back to the other end of the court. A teammate slapped him a high five. For a white guy, Shawn could hoop it up.

Andre, a left-handed black player for the Shirts, quickly brought the ball up-court the other way. Shawn dashed out to defend him, but Andre pulled up before Shawn could get there and drilled a three-point shot of his own. *SWISH!* Nothing but net.

Andre glared at Shawn. Unlike his opponent, he didn't scream anything provocative to raise the stakes of the game. Then again, he didn't need to. His silence spoke volumes. The intensity level rose a notch by itself. Some pickup games don't need a word.

A player from the Shirts, Mikey J., clapped his hands and crouched down low on the far side of the court. "Play some D now, boys. It's all tied up. Next hoop wins. Let's play some D!"

Cedric, his soft pink tongue dangling from his wide black mouth, brought the ball up-court for the Skins.

"I'm scorin' right now, ya hear?" Cedric boasted, talking some trash to Lorenzo.

"You ain't scoring here, punk," Lorenzo responded.

"I'm scorin' right here, right now, on *you*. Ya hear me?" Cedric taunted. "This game is over. We should stop right now and save you the embarrassment. Ya wanna give in?" Cedric offered as he dribbled the ball back and forth between his legs.

"Bring it on," Mikey J. cut in, crouching down even lower.

"You sure now?" Cedric asked, sweat flowing down his forehead.

"I said, bring it on," Mike answered again.

"All right. It's O-V-E-R."

With a big *whish* of his head and another front-to-back dribble, Cedric juked to the left, which created some space, leaving a teammate wide open on the wing for an easy fifteen-foot jumper. Cedric saw him, he saw him plain as day, but he didn't pass to him. Instead he drove down the lane, right into the teeth of the defense, where he was met by three determined defenders. Cedric tossed up a wild, off-balance running hook shot that missed by a mile and kicked long off the rim, bouncing out for an extended rebound. One of the Shirts got to the ball first and rifled a long, quick pass to Andre, who was breaking free from the pack in the other direction.

Andre snatched the ball in the open court and flashed to the rim. The only defender who could possibly catch him was Shawn. Shawn's feet left the ground and he flew through the air, trying to prevent the winning basket. There was a violent collision. Both players crashed to the ground. The basketball rolled around the rim. . . .

And dropped through the hoop.

"Game!" Andre barked as he quickly picked himself off the ground and pounced to a standing position directly over Shawn.

Shawn, still sprawled on the ground, amazed and disappointed, spit a goober in disgust. Andre looked at his right hand. It was bleeding from a small gash made sometime between the hard collision and the even harder fall. He glared again at Shawn.

"Nice touch," Shawn said to Andre in a mocking tone.

Andre squeezed his hand. Blood trickled down his palm.

"Damn right it was! Nice foul," Andre shot back.

Shawn jumped to his feet and got in Andre's face.

"Yeah, you were fouled," Shawn answered. "Fouled hard, too. So what?" Shawn got nose-to-nose with Andre. The other players slowly gathered around, forming a circle around the two as they stared each other down, white guy to black guy, eye-to-eye.

"Bust him in the jaw, Andre!" Cedric shouted.

Andre glared. Shawn didn't flinch.

"Go 'head, crank his ass!" Cedric roared again. "I got your back."

The tension built. Finally, Andre cracked a smile. Shawn smiled, too.

"Shut up, Ced, you fool," Andre said as he checked out the small cut on his hand again.

Shawn threw his arm warmly around Andre's

neck and they started walking off the court. "Sorry about that, buddy. But you know how it is. You gotta do what you gotta do on these courts. You all right?"

"I think so. You?" asked Andre.

"Me?" scoffed Shawn. "I'm indestructible; you know that."

Andre slowly extended the fingers of his right hand, made a fist, and then extended the fingers again. "Yeah, well, I'm not."

"That was a good finish," Shawn said in admiration as they picked their sweatshirts up off the bench by the fence.

"Was there ever a doubt?" Andre asked.

After a couple of see-ya-laters to the other players, Shawn scooped up the basketball and headed along with Andre to the water fountain. Cedric caught up from behind.

"You're lucky I wasn't back there on D, cause I woulda fouled you so hard, the ball would have been bruised," Cedric warned.

"If you were playing D?" Shawn responded with a quizzical look. "Man, Cedric, you never play D. Heck, you can't even spell D."

Andre and Shawn laughed and slapped a high five with each other. It was a special up-over-and-around high five that only a select few people in their inner circle knew. "And what kind of shot was that anyway, Ced?" Shawn added. "Mikey J. was wide open."

"Mikey J. was covered."

"He was wide open."

"I never saw him."

"Then how do you know he was covered?" Shawn asked, thinking he had Cedric cornered.

"'Cause I'm instinctual that way. I got a sixth sort of basketball sense. Like an extraterrestrial hoop awareness or something. It's just a gift."

"Yeah, sure, Ced. Always the star, huh?" Shawn replied, shaking his head.

"That's why they call me the Court Jester," Cedric said proudly.

"Man, that shot needed a Bible to go in," Andre remarked.

"And his head needs a bandage, too," Shawn added.

The three approached the water fountain for an after-basketball gulp of water. Cedric, ever the gentleman, darted in front of both Andre and Shawn to get the first sip.

Cedric pushed the button, closed his eyes, and waggled his big pink tongue in anticipation of a refreshing stream of cold H_2O.

It never came. Cedric's eyes popped open.

"Damn! I can't believe this thing's not working again," Cedric said with a look of disgust. "They can't do this to us!"

"Who is 'they,' Ced?" Andre asked as he and Shawn turned and started to walk away, resigned to the fact they would not be getting a drink either.

"Our oppressors, that's who," Cedric answered.

"Oh, I see," Andre answered, with a sarcastic nod of his head. "Our oppressors."

"That's right. Our oppressors!" Cedric replied.

"So write your congressman," Andre said as he put on his sweatshirt. Across the front, in small, simple print, the sweatshirt said THE HOOPSTER.

"You're the writer, you write him," Cedric retorted. "Tell him something like how the obvious racial prejudice shown by the water fountains in our neighborhood won't be tolerated anymore by us law-abiding, tax-paying, decent, hardworking folks."

"You're not a taxpayer," Shawn said.

"I was talking about your mom," Cedric answered with a smirk.

"Don't get me started on your bucktoothed momma," Shawn retorted.

"White people don't even have mommas,"

Cedric said. "They have mommies." Cedric began a high-pitched imitation of a white kid. "Mommy, Mommy, can I have a dollar? Mommy, Mommy, can I have a car? Mommy, Mommy, why do we have such small penises?"

"Okay, okay, you can talk trash about my momma," Shawn responded. "But don't smack about my penis."

"Whatever, Mr. Four-Inch."

Shawn paused.

"That's Mr. Four-*and-a-half* to you, buster," Shawn shot back. They all laughed.

"Damn, I'm thirsty," Cedric continued. "Andre, lemme borrow a dollar to get me a soda or something."

"Why don't you borrow a job?" Andre answered.

"I wouldn't need a job if the water fountains weren't racist," Cedric responded.

"If the water fountains are so prejudiced," Andre reasoned, "how come Shawn can't get a drink either? He's white."

"That's right. I'm white," Shawn said.

"And you're ugly, too," Cedric added. "But, unfortunately, you're also the unknowing victim of reverse discrimination."

"Reverse discrimination?" Andre repeated.

"Yeah, it sickens me," Cedric said. "Just sickens me."

Andre threw down his hands in futility and started to walk away. "Totally ridiculous."

"Don't you see? Nobody is safe." Cedric raised his voice like a preacher at the Sunday gospel. "We will not be turned away from the waters of the playground! We will not be deprived of the liquid that is our lifeblood!"

Andre turned to Shawn. "Let's get out of here."

"Our grandparents have tasted the wetness of the playground! The grandparents of our grandparents have tasted the wetness of the playground!" Cedric bellowed at the top of his lungs, stomping his foot like a modern-day Martin Luther King, Jr. "You cannot oppress us any longer! Our people will rise and drink from the water fountains again!" Andre and Shawn walked toward the parking lot, away from Cedric, to where Andre's blue Honda Accord was parked. It wasn't much of a car—the paint wasn't very shiny and the motor wasn't very fast—but to a seventeen-year-old like Andre, this car, his first, would always be a Rolls-Royce mixed with a Cadillac, sprinkled with a hint of Ferrari.

Andre opened the driver's-side door, proud of

the fact that he had saved up $3,000 of his own money for a set of wheels he could call his own. And for a teenager from Los Angeles, an automobile wasn't just a automobile. . . . It was freedom.

"Doesn't he need a ride?" Shawn asked as he climbed into the front seat.

"Nope, he just bought one," Andre answered.

"Cedric bought a car?" Shawn asked with a sideways look back toward Cedric.

"Cedric bought a bicycle," Andre answered.

Shawn and Andre turned around and watched Cedric unlock the most raggedy, beaten-up, hunk-of-junk bike any kid had ever owned. It was lime colored, with a bright orange security flag, and had a straw basket attached to the handlebars.

Cedric proudly mounted his new chariot and started to peddle away, still ranting about injustice.

"This day shall not go unremembered! Future generations will always know about the great water-fountain drought!"

The sight of Cedric on his new wheels was hypnotizing.

"He calls it his Pakistani Porsche," Andre informed Shawn.

"You can read history many times!" Cedric

pontificated. "But you can only write it once! Listen to what I say, people! Hear my words! See my actions!" Cedric chanted as he rode off into the distance.

"Your cousin is crazy," Shawn finally said to Andre.

"You should talk?" Andre said.

Shawn flipped open the glove box of Andre's car, looking for some tasty tunes to pump in the stereo. "What's that supposed to mean?"

"It means, I don't need you knocking at my window at three A.M. to see if I want to go throw snowballs at the paperboy," Andre answered. He checked the gas gauge. It was almost empty. "Got any coinage?" he asked. "I need some gas."

"What are you complaining about?" Shawn answered. "You were still up."

"There aren't any snowballs in the middle of summer," Andre answered.

"Up writing like you do every night. Type. Type. Type. Work. Work. Work. *Blah. Blah. Blah.*" Shawn said the "blah" part with extra oomph.

"Plus," Andre added as he scrounged for some change in his ashtray. "You guys don't even get the newspaper. Now, how much money do you have?"

"Yeah, I know. I just steal the sports page from the neighbors' house."

"And don't think my pops doesn't know it's you, either," Andre shot back.

"Aw, I always bring it back," Shawn answered with his irresistible grin. "Besides, someone has got to keep an eye on the next Ernest Hummingbird."

"Hemingway."

"Whatever."

Andre looked Shawn straight in the eye. His search for cash had been fruitless, and now it was time for one of those hard questions that sometimes has to be asked of close friends who have been mooching for far too much, for far too long. "So, how much money do you have?"

Shawn knew the tone and fell silent. It was time to pony up.

"Sorry, dude, I'm tapped," he responded with a carefree shrug of his shoulders and went back to flipping through the CD case. Andre peered at Shawn, wondering how he could possibly have so much nerve.

"Now, home, Ernest," Shawn said as he loaded some hard beats into the face of the car stereo.

Andre heaved a sigh and turned the ignition key. The music blasted from the stereo speakers like a surge of ice water ripping through Andre's ears. Shawn, loving every second of it, turned up the tunes even louder, ready to blow the subwoofers straight out of the backseat.

Andre straightened his rearview mirror, put the car in gear, and wondered how on earth he had ever ended up with this guy as his best friend.

II

"Hi, Mom!" Shawn called out as he slammed through the front door of his house. It was a nice house with spick-and-span floors, a comfy couch, and a hearty long-leafed plant sitting right beside the door. To the left of the plant pot was where Shawn liked to kick off his shoes and leave them lying like wounded soldiers, casualties in the battle against cleanliness.

Dumph! His sneakers landed with a thud. Andre politely closed the front door behind him as he entered. Shawn paused and sniffed the air.

Meat loaf, he mouthed to Andre with obvious disapproval, then walked to the kitchen, where Mrs. Vincent, Shawn's thin, sturdy mother, was cooking dinner.

Shawn yanked open the refrigerator door, pulled out a jug of cranberry juice, and drank straight from the bottle. Mrs. Vincent watched her son gulp down a giant swallow, a portion of which streamed down the side of his cheek, but didn't say a word. She had lost the "No drinking straight from the container!" battle many years before.

"Ah, that's good. Here," Shawn said as he passed the jug to Andre. "Any more cookies, Mom?"

Shawn wiped the red juice from his cheek with the sleeve of his T-shirt, which, considering how filthy the shirt already was, didn't really affect its overall wearability at all. Andre paused and held the jug in his hand, not yet taking a drink. Shawn, not paying attention to Andre, poked and prodded in the fridge, looking for something he could quickly jam into his mouth. The only prerequisite for the food he was searching for was that it be ready to eat, scrumptious, and *not* healthy. If his mother would have approved of it, he didn't want it.

"Ain't we got any more cookies?" Shawn said, butchering the English language along the way for her benefit. He ransacked the back of the refrigerator, shoving aside the eight-month-old bottle of pickles no one ever ate.

"Why don't you have an apple?" Mrs. Vincent responded.

"Aw, Mom," Shawn replied. A piece of fruit was such a *mom* thing to suggest. Mrs. Vincent was a crafty mother though, and the best Shawn could find was a leftover double-stuffed baked potato from the previous night's dinner. Although the laws of physics would usually disallow inserting such a large object into one's face without biting, Shawn, ever the rebel, managed to plow the whole potato into his oral cavity simply by using the force of his fingers and that ever-flexible tool, teenage jaws.

"Maybe Andre would like a glass?" Mrs. Vincent prompted. Though she wore an apron, Mrs. Vincent never thought of herself as one of those moms who wears aprons. But she was. They all are.

"*Nrrmm-ugmm,*" Shawn replied, chewing and swallowing and waving his hands as if the idea were ridiculous. "Cumrron, drink up," Shawn continued between gulps. "I want to show you my latest."

Andre looked over at Mrs. Vincent, shrugged, and took a sip of juice straight from the container. Mrs. Vincent shook her head and smiled, thinking the same thought that moms all over this world have thought for thousands of years: Boys will be boys.

"*Brrrrgghhuup!*" Shawn belched.

Shawn's mom threw him a look.

"Excuse me," Shawn offered mildly when he saw her glare. His burp was obviously louder and more disgusting than even he thought it would be. There was no real way to apologize for something that rude. And when the smell hit, Mrs. Vincent was even less amused, though Shawn chivalrously tried to fan it away.

"Andre, honey," Mrs. Vincent asked as the boys started to exit the kitchen. "Will you be having dinner with us tonight?"

"Thanks, but I don't think so," Andre replied. "I think my mom is expecting me."

"Well, as you know, you're more than welcome."

"I know. Thank you anyway, but—"

"But he's supposed to get home so that his mother can make sure that he gets a decent meal in him. Something that he likes to eat," Shawn said. "Something that's not m-e-a-t l-o-a-f."

"You love meat loaf," Mrs. Vincent said, without raising her eyes. She continued cutting vegetables.

"No, I don't," Shawn complained.

"Yes, you do," she answered.

"Mom," Shawn said in his most serious tone. "No, I don't. Maybe when I was like three or four years old and you used to dress me up in dorky sailor suits you got the wrong idea about me and meat loaf. But I want to tell you something right now that I hope you never forget. I do not love meat loaf. I do not even like meat loaf. As a matter of fact, Mom, I hate meat loaf."

Mrs. Vincent bent over and checked the dish in the oven. "You love meat loaf."

"I hate meat loaf!"

"You love it."

"I hate it!"

"I like meat loaf," Andre interjected.

"So you stay for dinner," Shawn responded.

"I can't. My mom's making barbecued chicken."

"You see? You see?" Shawn pleaded. "Andre's mom is making barbecued chicken."

"Andre loves barbecued chicken," Mrs. Vincent answered as she poked a fork at her dish. "And you love meat loaf."

Shawn threw up his hands and marched out of the kitchen, the same thought running through his head that has run through the heads of sons all over the world for thousands of years: My mother is driving me crazy.

"Just a few minutes till we eat, Shawny," Mrs. Vincent called out for good measure.

Shawn's room was a mess. The bed was unmade, half-filled soda cans were abandoned all over the place, and scattered phone numbers, candy wrappers, envelopes, and miscellaneous papers lay all about.

Most notably, though, there were clothes. Dirty clothes. Clean clothes. Piles of clothes. Everywhere! Only Shawn could tell the difference between which clothes smelled sweet and which ones stank. He did this by applying the stench test: he smelled the armpits or crotch of the item, and if he didn't shrink back in horror with his nose hairs on fire, it meant it was clean enough to wear. Shawn's mother, of course, would have said that everything was fit for the washing machine—or better yet, the incinerator—but Shawn would have disagreed violently.

More noticeable than the clothes or the mess, though, were the walls and other eye-catching "objects" scattered about the room. There were artist's canvases, pieces of clay, paintbrushes, putty knives, paints, and all sorts of other artistic utensils scattered everywhere. On the walls hung only original works by Shawn. Some were bright and jumped out at the viewer. Others were a bit more subdued and refined. It was a hodgepodge of colors, subjects, energies, and inspirations flowing everywhere, with the only real unifying theme being that they were all very skillfully executed. It was obvious that while Shawn's room was a wreck, it had been wrecked by a person with a great deal of talent.

"Check this out," Shawn said as he made his way

to the corner where a sheet hung over something large and bulging. Shawn turned on a lamp that served double duty as a spotlight. "It's my latest."

Shawn slowly removed the sheet. Underneath was a sculpture . . . of a naked woman. Well, not really naked. Bare breasted. And pretty. And young. And she was biting her fingernail with a thoughtful, almost pensive look on her face. "She was nude and she was pondering," Shawn said.

The sculpture's lifelike depth of character might have startled a stranger, but not Andre, because he was quite familiar with the extent of his best friend's talent. Shawn was an artist with abilities well beyond his years, and art was the only thing Shawn seemed to really care about at school. Instead of drooling over the piece's excellence, though, Andre thoughtfully studied the work over before giving his opinion.

"What do you call it?" Andre inquired after a moment more.

"I don't know yet," Shawn answered. "Maybe *Meat-loaf Mother*."

"That's not funny," Andre said. They both laughed.

"Her nostrils aren't even," Andre noted.

"What?" Shawn replied.

"Her nostrils aren't even. One's bigger than the other."

"You don't know what you're talking about," Shawn shot back as he slid over to take a closer look.

"See? Her left air passage looks like a manhole cover," Andre said, exaggerating just a little bit.

"What are you talking about?" Shawn replied with a tinge of anger in his voice. "I spent a lot of time on her nostrils."

They both carefully looked them over.

"Nope. Definitely looks like she could snort up a quarter without even turning it sideways," Andre said. "Who did you use for a subject?"

"Jennifer Rhodes."

"Jenny Rhodes?" Andre said with a combination of surprise and admiration. "Wow, how'd you ever get her to take off her shirt in this pigsty of a bedroom?"

"It's all in the name of art," Shawn replied with a sly smile.

"You're a hound," Andre responded. "Are Jenny's nostrils really uneven? I never noticed."

"The nostrils are not uneven," Shawn answered. "You don't know what you're talking about."

"Look at that one," Andre said, pointing to the left nostril. "It's all smacked up."

"It is not!"

"I'm tellin' ya, her left olfactory orifice thingy is whack, dude. I bet it's because she used to eat her boogers in second grade."

"Jenny didn't eat her boogers in second grade. That was Frannie Moscowitz."

"Nuh-uh, Frannie used to pick the cheese from her belly button and sniff it in science class."

"You have the worst memory," Shawn protested. "Frannie Moscowitz ate her boogers, Maria Songas liked to breathe her own farts, and Pauline Shamato smelled her belly-button cheese."

"If Frannie Moscowitz ate her boogers, then why is Jenny's nose hole the size of a cantaloupe?"

"Her nose hole is not the size of a cantaloupe, you peckerhead!" Shawn shot back as he tossed a reeking sock at Andre's head, just barely missing.

"Face it, dude, you chose a booger-picking model and it threw off your dimensions." Andre calmly walked over and scooped up a bit of moist clay. "I mean, look, I'm no sculptor, but all you probably have to do is take some of this wet clay, pretend it is a booger and carefully put it back inside Jenny's nose. After all the green she's yanked out of that schnoz, I'm sure her face will be thanking you."

"Are you insane?" Shawn hollered as he jumped up on the bed. "This is a work of art!"

"And then when this new, gooder booger is dry you can—" Andre cut himself off in midsentence. The bedroom door swung open. It was Mrs. Vincent.

Unfortunately Shawn was too worked up about Andre's advice and the sculpture to notice, and instead of shutting up like Andre, he raised his voice.

"You want to see a gooder booger? I'll show you a gooder booger!" Shawn shouted. "How's this for a stroll down memory lane?" Suddenly, Shawn jammed his index finger three inches up his nose, lifted his shirt, and started digging for belly-button lint while bouncing up and down on his bed making fart sounds.

"Look at me! Look at me! *Frrrpppp! Frrrpppp!* I am a nose-picking, belly-button-licking fart smeller!" Shawn bounced even higher. "*Frrrpppp! Frrrpppp!* Look at me! Look at me!"

Andre dropped his head and covered his eyes. Shawn, after another moment of bouncing up and down, sensed something wasn't quite right. He turned.

"Uh, hi, Mom."

It took Mrs. Vincent about sixty-seven hours to respond. "Dinner will be ready in five minutes," she said softly.

Shawn quietly took his finger out of his nose, lowered his shirt over his stomach, and climbed down from the bed to cover the sculpture with a sheet. "Oh, okay."

"Are you sure you don't want to stay for dinner, Andre?" Mrs. Vincent asked, her voice still low.

"No, thank you, Mrs. Vincent," Andre answered. "I have some work to do tonight, anyway."

"At least someone has some real ambition around here," Mrs. Vincent commented in a not-so-subtle tone.

"Come on, Mom," Shawn replied. "You know I only want to go to art school next fall."

"Art school is not college," she answered without looking at him, and then continued her conversation with Andre. "Are things going well for you down at the magazine, Andre?" she inquired.

"Oh, sure, sure," Andre replied. "Things are fine. I mean, I just had my third article rejected by the editor yesterday, but other than having every dream I ever had in the world shattered, things are pretty good."

"Oh, sorry to hear that, Andre. But remember, you're interning for a fairly big-time publication now," Mrs. Vincent responded. "It's not all going to come at once."

"He's getting paid, Mom. It's not one of those free things. They think he's good," Shawn said with an edge in his voice, defending his buddy.

"Yeah, I dunno. They say it goes with the business, but I've never faced so much rejection in all my life. 'No. No. No.' It's all I ever hear. It's so competitive. And the big boss is like some kind of dragon."

"That's what they mean by 'paying your dues,' Andre," Mrs. Vincent said, glancing at Shawn to see if he had any other smart-aleck remarks to offer.

He didn't.

"Yeah, I guess. I just keep plugging along, you know, hoping and waiting for my chance to do something one day. Something more than gathering research and photocopying, that is."

"Well, you keep at it, honey, you'll get your chance to shine," Mrs. Vincent said. "We all do, Andre. We all do. Isn't that right, Shawn?"

"Yes, Mom," he replied, without looking up.

"Oh, Shawn . . ."

Shawn raised his eyes.

"Meat loaf."

His head sank low again. "Yes, Mom," Shawn answered. Mrs. Vincent surveyed the mess in the room. Andre had the feeling that even though she really wanted to pick things up and straighten things out, she knew it would be a complete waste of time, so she fought her instincts and left.

"She always givin' me grief," Shawn said as he turned off the lamp that lit the sculpture. "Hey, you think she heard us, you know, about the farting and stuff?" Shawn asked in a serious tone.

Andre paused.

"Nawwww!" they both blurted out at the same time with a big laugh, knowing quite well that she had heard every word.

"Eat your meat loaf. I'm going home," Andre responded as he headed out of Shawn's room and toward the front door.

Shawn followed right behind. "Wanna go out tonight? I'm supposed to meet Vicki and—"

"I can't. I've got some stuff to do."

"You haven't even heard what we're gonna do yet."

"Sorry, just can't."

"Whoever heard of a summer job with home-work?" Shawn shot back. "People our age should always become camp counselors, like me. I joke around with kids all day, have fun, get exercise—"

"So this could be like a career thing?" Andre asked.

"What are you, my mom? Besides, I meet a lot

of girls," Shawn added, taunting Andre. "How many girls do you meet at your job?" he asked.

"I meet girls," Andre said, lying to Shawn.

"Yeah, ugly ones maybe," Shawn scoffed. "Seriously, your writing is getting in the way of your social life, dude. You, my friend, need a woman."

Andre opened up the front door and stepped outside. "Oh, I do?"

"Yes, you do," Shawn told him. "Hey, I don't know why I didn't think of this before. I know the perfect girl for you. No, I'm serious. Come by the camp tomorrow during your lunchtime and I'll set you up with this totally hot babe. She'd be awesome for you."

Andre looked at him suspiciously. He knew better than to trust Shawn.

"Naw, I'm serious. She's great. She's pretty. She's smart. She likes school. And she's really fun, too."

"I'm sure," Andre responded.

"Well . . . there is one thing," Shawn admitted.

"What's that, she picks her nose?"

"No," Shawn responded in a serious tone. "The girl I am thinking about, well, she, yeah, I'm sure that she . . ." Shawn shook his head. "Yeah," Shawn said more to himself than to Andre. "I'm sure it would be fine."

"What'd be fine? What's wrong with her?" asked Andre, his curiosity piqued.

"Well . . ."

"Shawwwwn," Andre said in a low voice.

"Well, dude . . . she's only nine," he replied as a big smile spread across his face.

"I'm outta here!" Andre said, and stormed off. He should have known better than to listen to Shawn. Yet still, he had fallen for it.

"If you change your mind, you know where to find me," Shawn said, following Andre to his car. "Think about it. She's open-minded, sensitive, a youthful spirit. And she gets an allowance, too."

"Think about noses, buddy," Andre said as he climbed into the car.

"Well, you know what they say. You can pick your friends and you can pick your nose. . . ."

"But you can't pick your friend's nose," Andre replied. They both laughed.

And before parting ways for the evening, they exchanged a special up-over-and-around high five.

III

Dressed in a red sweater and pleated black slacks, Andre felt confident because he knew he looked good. It wasn't arrogance, though. Andre cared about the way he dressed, had a strong, athletic build, and knew he looked sharp in nice clothing. He also knew that when he looked sharp, he felt sharp. That's why he always ironed his Hoopster T-shirts before going to play basketball, and that's why he always made it a point to look elegant whenever he dressed for the office. And by magazine-office standards, Andre was a regular Rudolph Valentino.

Andre's desk at *Affairs* magazine wasn't really any sort of desk at all. That's because *Affairs* magazine wasn't quite in the big league ballpark of periodicals like *Newsweek*, *Vanity Fair,* or *Time*, though it was trying. One of the many ways management kept costs down was to provide one fax machine and one photocopy machine for all seventy-three employees, including the boss. Another was to pay Andre with free pizza on Fridays, a virtually invisible credit on the magazine's masthead each month, and a lower hourly wage than most dishwashers made for scrubbing dirty pots in the dank kitchens of local restaurants. Such is the life of aspiring literary stars. But as Shawn had noted to his mom, at least Andre was making a little cash, and that counted for something.

The part of the fax table that the fax machine didn't take up was Andre's official desk. All day long he had people walking up to, and through, his work space as they sent, received, and grumbled about their faxes. The fax machine constantly beeped as well. It was an annoying, high-pitched beep, whose sole purpose was to signal to users that the machine was in use.

And it was always in use.

If that weren't enough to drive a person crazy, Andre's desk was right around the corner from the photocopy machine, which was always whizzing and whirring and misfiring. There were perks, though. Because Andre's workspace was just out of view of people using the copier, Andre got the benefit of hearing all kinds of private standing-at-the-copier conversations. Sometimes people at the machine gossiped about their colleagues, sometimes people gossiped about sex, and sometimes people gossiped about sex with their colleagues. People did strange things when they were alone, as well. Andre took a lot of pleasure from hearing people try to smooth-talk the copy machine when it was being persnickety. They'd say things like, "Come on, sugar pie, make a copy for Daddy." Other times they simply cursed the hell out of it. Occasionally, the copier even got kicked in the groin. Like the rest of us, it would groan.

With seventy-three employees and just one set of office machines, constant use was the order of the day. Constant use meant constant beeping, buzzing, slamming, feeding, mumbling, sneezing, and pounding. Andre's spot was far and away the worst location on the whole floor to have a work space.

And Andre loved every inch of it.

He wasn't worried about noises and lack of desk space and interruptions. Andre was hungrier than that. He was a writer. Maybe not yet an official writer, because making photocopies and fetching resource materials wasn't exactly the same thing as penning articles for a major magazine, but at least he worked where writers worked and that was good enough to fill his head with the buzz of ambition. He also knew that with only one set of office machines (and there were two paths to the photocopier but only one path to the fax) everyone who worked for

Affairs would eventually have to cross before him. With his sunny smile and friendly disposition, it wasn't three weeks before he was on a first-name basis with each of the seventy-two other employees, including the big boss.

"Knicks gonna do it this year, Andre?" Joseph, the ad sales guy with the beard, asked Andre as he waited for his fax from a guy who owned a car dealership.

"Not without any outside shooting," Andre responded.

"I'm telling you, it's the year of the Knicks," Joseph countered.

"Naw, the Knicks can't even run a screen and roll without dribbling the ball off somebody's foot. My dark-horse pick this year is the Clippers. Watch for them to make some noise in the playoffs." Andre's dark horse every year was the Clippers, but Joseph didn't know that.

Joseph chuckled and walked away. Not fifteen seconds later Ellen ran up to Andre looking frazzled. Ellen was a freelance writer who had been lobbying for a staff position for the past three months. She was a short, ditzy Jewish woman who always tried hard but inevitably seemed to be in the wrong place at the wrong time, saying the wrong thing.

"Andre, do you have any clue where the *Almanac of the American People* is?" Ellen asked. "I need a stat on the number of Americans with type two diabetes."

"Third shelf down from the back-issue rack," Andre replied, "but you should try the *Encyclopaedia of Health and Behavior* first."

Ellen looked at him skeptically. She wasn't much for new things.

"It's more current and easier to use," Andre added to allay her fears.

"Oh, okay. And that's . . . ?" Ellen had no idea where that book was either.

"Below the phone books," Andre said.

"Right," Ellen said. "Thanks."

"Or better yet you could—" Andre stopped himself in midsentence and changed what he was about to say. "No, try the encyclopedia first. If that doesn't have what you want, come back. I have another idea." The other idea Andre had, but was reluctant to mention, was using the Internet, but he knew that putting Ellen on the net was like putting her on roller skates in San Francisco—she wasn't going to make it very far and there was a chance of someone or something being damaged.

"It's all wrong, Ed. I can't run this." Andre

heard a deep, booming voice getting louder as it approached.

"What's wrong with it?" Andre heard Ed respond.

"To start with, it's as hollow as an empty Easter egg." The voice was unmistakable. It belonged to a plump, fifty-three-year-old balding man from Chicago who had been in the magazine business since he was eleven. His name was Michael Huntington Jarvin and he was the editor-in-chief of *Affairs* magazine. "This story has no depth, no feeling. It's like I'm reading a scientific journal when it's supposed to be a human-interest piece. I want sentiment and revelation, Ed. Not economic analysis."

Ed's voice softly answered, "Uh-huh."

"Where's the real understanding of the situation? Where's the heart? What we're talking about are racial tensions and the forces that propel them. You've given me nothin' here." Mr. Jarvin wasn't a guy who minced words. "No compassion. No outrage. No understanding. No nothin'."

"Well, maybe I didn't see it," responded Ed. Andre could picture him running his fingers through his light brown hair.

Ed and Mr. Jarvin approached the photocopy machine from the back, the side from which they couldn't see Andre.

Andre tried to pretend he was doing something significant, and though he had a mound of things he could have been doing, the most important thing at the time seemed to be listening in on a heated conversation that was only getting hotter.

"Listen, Mr. Jarvin, I'm a good writer and I have done some very good work for this magazine. But frankly"—Ed leaned in after a quick glance around to make sure no one else was listening—"I found this assignment to be tedious. I mean, I just don't get 'those' kind of people."

There was an awkward, stilted silence. Once again Andre thought about how much he loved his desk—and how much of an idiot Ed was.

"Ed, I ain't gonna run this," Mr. Jarvin said in a very strident tone. A rustle of paper indicated he was handing Ed back his work. "Maybe I'll use Susan's piece on overfishing the Pacific, I dunno. But I do know that I am not going to run this. It is . . ." Mr. Jarvin took a moment to search for the right word. *"Inferior."*

Like a chastised schoolboy, Ed left. Andre imagined that Mr. Jarvin was rubbing his chubby hand over the big wrinkles on his brow when he heard him throw open the cupboard door to grab a bottle of aspirin off the shelf. (Andre's office was also the company medicine cabinet.) Andre quietly listened to him pour himself a cup of water from the company water cooler only steps away.

"Mr. Jarvin," Ed said. He must have turned around and reentered the commons area. "There is something else I would like to say."

"Yes," replied Mr. Jarvin.

Andre leaned in a bit closer.

"I just wanted to say that, well, personally, I don't have any pity for those type of people. And I don't think that I am alone when I say that either. It's not like I am oppressing them personally. I mean, I believe in America, land of the free, home of the brave, and all of that crap. But as far as I am concerned, equal opportunity does exist in the USA. No matter what color you are."

Andre couldn't resist taking a peek. Mr. Jarvin looked Ed squarely in the eye and then tossed his headache pills down the back of his throat. Mr. Jarvin had the look of a man who took headache pills often. Guys like Ed were the reason. Andre pulled back out of potential sight.

"You know, you hear about these athletes, these movie stars, these hip-hop rappers making millions of dollars, and it doesn't matter what color they are. They earn their money based on their ability to perform at their jobs. Well," Ed continued in a dignified tone, "I work hard at my job and earn my money, too. I went to school, I found employment and I climbed the ladder. Nobody put me where I am today because of the color of my skin—or the color my skin is not. Heck, I earned what I have."

Mr. Jarvin was silent.

"And so can they," Ed added for good measure.

Mr. Jarvin remained silent. After another moment, however, he spoke.

"You finished?" he asked with a raised eyebrow.

Ed took a moment before he answered. He felt righteous in what he had said and seemed to believe he had made a good, solid, justifiable point. Ed screwed up his courage and responded. "Yes, I'm finished."

Andre heard Mr. Jarvin take another sip of his water, crumple his paper cup, and toss it into the wastepaper basket.

"Look, Ed, if your personal beliefs conflict with your professional obligations, I can understand that." Ed must have felt a warm wave of comfort run through him. He had been in the right. Mr. Jarvin wasn't an unfeeling, leathery old man after all. In fact, Ed must have been thinking, he was a pretty good boss. Yeah, he was tough, but when a guy hit him with a logical point, at least he listened to what he had to say.

"But." At the sound of the word *but* Andre knew all of Ed's warm, cozy, nice feelings had vanished. "There comes a time in life where you gotta take a stand for what you believe in or step aside. I don't give a donkey's ding-a-ling whether or not you believe a segment of black America is frustrated and feels oppressed. It's got no relevance to me now. The time to come forward and tell me these things was *five weeks ago* when I gave you the damned assignment! Your job was to come up with a fresh angle on an old problem in an intelligent and gripping way. And, Ed"—Mr. Jarvin paused for dramatic effect—"you totally failed to do this."

It was Ed who was now silent.

"What makes this business work is either heart-felt passion or keen perception. Faking it won't do. Now call me on Monday and I'll see if I feel like scraping you up something different to work on."

Andre heard Ed walk away. Mr. Jarvin stayed where he was. Andre heard a muttered "That damned Ed," or something to that effect. Except for the quiet hum of the photocopy machine, silence thickly filled the air. Andre sensed that even the copy machine seemed scared to step out of line. Everyone in the office instinctively seemed to know to stay away for a few minutes.

Andre, himself, felt tense and was frozen to his seat. If he moved he might make a sound that would let Mr. Jarvin know he had been right there, sneakily listening around the corner the whole time to his conversation. That would not be good. Andre sat as still as a closed door.

"I found it, Andre!" Ellen burst around the corner, holding the encyclopedia. "Right where you said it would be. Thank goodness, too. For a minute I thought I was going to have to go on the Internet."

Mr. Jarvin peeped around the corner and, sure enough, there was Andre looking as guilty as guilty could look.

"Oh, Mr. Jarvin, I—I—I didn't see you there," Ellen stuttered. "I was, I was just saying thanks to Andre. He's such a big help and, yes, I think that I am going to ask him to help me on . . . on a bigger project next time. Maybe he can research statistics on ambulance accidents and I can show him how to write a strong opening paragraph." She was obviously frazzled. "With a strong opening sentence."

Mr. Jarvin further wrinkled his already wrinkled brow. It didn't take a mind reader to know the thought running through his head was, What the hell are you talking about, woman? Ellen became even more nervous upon seeing this expression and made the mistake of continuing.

"Not for the magazine, but I will help him, you know, like the way a tree forms from the seed of a small writer. I'll help him like that, kind of."

Ellen replayed her words over in her head sixty-six times during the next weekend and, after a great deal of reflection, she determined that the worst aspect of everything she had said was ending her final sentence with a preposition. After all, she was speaking to a magazine editor.

"I'll be going now," Ellen said meekly, and then left Andre alone with Jarvin.

Mr. Jarvin slowly scanned Andre's makeshift desk. There were books, files, pens, highlighters, and lots of notepads with lots of writing. Though he had probably passed it a hundred times, this was the first time Mr. Jarvin was really *seeing* Andre's desk. Andre felt the weight of the Mr. Jarvin's assessment in his throat like a piece of unchewed steak.

"Andre," boomed Mr. Jarvin. "Come into my office."

Mr. Jarvin turned and walked away. Andre gulped, but the steak didn't go down. He should have known better than to eavesdrop.

Picking some imaginary lint from his sweater, Andre stood up and vowed to take it like a man. He didn't deserve to be fired over this, he thought to himself. He worked too darned hard at what he did and he always put forth his best effort, even when he was assigned to do things that required no brains or talent whatsoever. He remembered the time he had called thirty-seven gas stations to find out why all of them charged nine tenths of a cent extra for a gallon of gas when the smallest denomination a person could pay was one whole cent. Everyone in the world understood it was a ploy to rip off the public but, still, he had made the calls. And there was the time he had stayed until 11:15 P.M. on a Friday night, making sure a thank-you package had been received in Thailand by a reporter from Bangkok who had helped out *Affairs* with a piece on the opium-growing Golden Triangle. Everyone told Andre it was just a simple thank-you and that he could deal with any problems on Monday, but Andre had stayed anyway, long into the night. Now he was about to have his first, and potentially last, real conversation about his job performance with the big boss, and it was about something stupid. (All of the rejection notices Andre had received were filtered down through simple, unencouraging memos from Mr. Jarvin, which simply read "Bzzzt." Mr. Jarvin liked the word *no* a great deal, and seemed to use it all the time in conversation, but it appeared that he liked to write the word *bzzzt* even more, especially when it came to assessing Andre's work.)

Andre pulled up his sleepy socks, hitched up his pants, and made his way to the office of the editor as requested.

"Close the door and take a seat," Mr. Jarvin said as he put a half-smoked cigar into his mouth.

Andre did as he was told.

"You've been doing a nice job around here, Andre," Mr. Jarvin began.

"I didn't mean to eavesdrop, Mr. Jarvin," he began in his own defense. "Well, that's not true. I won't lie to you. I was eavesdropping. I did mean to. But I work hard and I really like it here and I think it is a bit excessive to let me go just because I didn't make my presence known by coughing or something like that. I mean that *is* my desk area."

"Let you go?" Mr. Jarvin interjected.

"Okay, I guess I could have gotten up or done something to let you know I was there," Andre continued, "but I never thought the conversation was going to turn to—"

"Wait. Wait. Slow down," Mr. Jarvin interrupted. "You're not being canned, Andre. Relax."

"Oh, I'm not," said Andre. "Well . . . thanks."

"Don't thank me. You're smart, enthusiastic, a hard worker. Things like that don't go unnoticed around here," Mr. Jarvin said as he readjusted the cigar in his mouth. "At least, not forever they don't," he added with a chuckle. Mr. Jarvin may have been a hard-ass, but he had a good, hearty laugh.

Andre looked around and noticed the books on the shelves, the folders stuffed with papers piled on chairs where people might have sat, and a picture of Mr. Jarvin in an ill-fitting suit shaking the hand of the vice president of the United States. While Andre scanned the office, Mr. Jarvin scanned Andre. He seemed to be mulling something over in his head. Finally, Mr. Jarvin appeared to come to a conclusion.

"Hell, Andre, it's showtime. You wanted it, you got it. I'm gonna give you your shot at writing a feature-length article for this magazine. Whaddaya think of that?"

"Well, I—"

"Now, just hold off a minute, Andre, and don't get your underpants all knotty. I guess you heard a bit of what happened between Ed and me a minute ago, but don't get the wrong idea. Forget Ed. He's a putz," Mr. Jarvin said. "Then again, always remember, we all have our shortcomings, Andre. All of us."

"Yeah, I guess so," Andre replied.

"Good. Now, I want you to write an article for us on racism," Mr. Jarvin continued as he rose from his seat. "I want it to be about prejudice against people of color. Hell, against people without color. Just about people, that's what I want. It's like I know what I want, but I don't know what I want, you know what I mean? I want you to write something for us from your heart."

"Well, I don't think—"

"Now, I know, it's very weighty subject matter, especially for a young writer, but I want you to try it. Give it some oomph. Develop your own slant, create your own take, let's just see what ya come up with."

"Mr. Jarvin, I—"

"All the media coverage nowadays is too—too sensational, too extreme," Mr. Jarvin proceeded without letting Andre get a word in edgewise. "Pictures of ghettoes, the projects, drugs, gangs, guns—always the extremes. This stuff sells, but what's at the heart of the matter? Hell, I dunno. Who does know? Maybe you know. Maybe it's worth a chance to find out. I just want somebody who can write something a bit closer to the core of the matter. More meaningful, you know? Do ya have a sense of what I'm talkin' about, Andre?"

"I think that—"

"Good, 'cause I would just like to find something, something honest." Mr. Jarvin sat back down and rolled the cigar through his mouth, lost in thought. "Yeah, honest."

"May I say something, Mr. Jarvin?" Andre asked. "I mean, without losing my job?"

"Of course, Andre. I don't work like that. Go right ahead."

"I feel—"

"That's enough—get out, you're *fired*!" Mr. Jarvin shouted as he leaped forward in his chair. Andre jumped back, startled, but before he could respond, Mr. Jarvin was laughing that good, hearty laugh of his. "Just goofin' around, Andre. Go 'head."

Andre faked a half-smile, but what he had to say was more pressing to him than a joke right then. "I am respectfully going to have to turn you down, Mr. Jarvin. I'm not the right person for this assignment."

"And what makes you so damned sure of that?" asked Jarvin. "Look, I have spent a hell of a long time in this business and I—"

"Now, please, Mr. Jarvin, let me finish what I have to say." Andre's sudden forcefulness surprised Mr. Jarvin. Frankly, it surprised Andre, too. Mr. Jarvin's natural reaction would have been to bark right back. After all, he was a man who very few people ever growled at, and if they did, he made sure to let them know he was the biggest dog in the park. But despite his initial inclination to snap back at Andre, Mr. Jarvin paused, nodded his head up and down, and relaxed back into his chair as if to say, *My apologies. Go right ahead, Andre.* Of course he didn't say these words, but not chewing Andre's face off meant just about the same thing.

Andre began slowly. "Thank you. Now, first, I want you to know that I really want to write for this magazine one day. I really do. It's my dream to become a professional writer. But I'm not sure about this chance you are giving me. Just because I am black doesn't mean I know the cure for racism."

"Now, hold on, Andre—"

"No, no, wait, please don't interrupt me. You see, prejudice, bigotry, racism, it's ugly stuff. But to tell you the truth, I don't really think it affects me personally all that much. I mean, I go to school, get good grades, my parents have jobs, I own a car, you know? Don't get me wrong, racism is a very important topic, Mr. Jarvin, but if it is going to be discussed seriously, it needs to be treated properly. You can't just throw me an assignment because I'm a brotha," Andre said. "No offense," he quickly added. "But does what I am saying make sense?"

Mr. Jarvin rubbed his chin. "I hear what you're saying, Andre."

"Good. And thanks, I guess." Andre politely stood up from his chair and started walking toward the door. "I mean, it was nice of you to consider me."

"Have a first draft ready in four weeks."

"Excuse me?" Andre asked as he turned back around.

"I said have a first draft ready—"

"Oh, I heard what you said, but I don't think you heard what I said, Mr. Jarvin."

"Of course I did, Andre. And that is precisely why I am even more confident now than I was before that I have chosen the right writer for this job. Don't sell yourself short. You're good. You've earned this shot."

Andre shook his head in disbelief.

"And that was a nice little speech, too," Mr. Jarvin offered. "I'm looking forward to your article. Would you mind closing the door on the way out?"

"But, Mr. Jarvin—"

"No *buts*, Andre!" Mr. Jarvin roared as he exploded out of his seat. "Take it from a guy who started at the bottom. I am offering you an opportunity here, a fantastic opportunity, and it is not because you are black, so *bzzzt*, you can put that excuse to rest. It is because you are qualified *as a writer*."

A moment of silence passed between them.

"You owe it to yourself to take this shot, Andre. You're not doing this for me, you're doing this for you. I'm just going to get the benefit. And I have a feeling it is going to be great. Great. Now, you have four weeks. I'm sure you'll do a bang-up job. Aren't you?"

"Well," Andre responded. "I mean, sure, I guess."

"Of course you are. Now, take some courage, mix in some faith, and approach this assignment like it very well could be the thing that leads you to your destiny," Mr. Jarvin advised as he sat back in his chair and rolled the cigar between his lips. "Everyone has a destiny. But you have to claim it."

Andre weighed the proposition in his head. "My own angle, right?"

Mr. Jarvin took the cigar out of his mouth. He knew he had Andre hooked. "You have four weeks. Put it together in the standard format, using—"

"Oh, I know the format," Andre said eagerly.

Mr. Jarvin smiled at his sudden enthusiasm. "I'm sure you do."

Andre turned to leave the office again, this time with a bounce in his stride.

"Oh, Andre, I almost forgot," Mr. Jarvin called out. "Remember that piece we ran on magicians a few issues back? Seems attendance at the Forum Club is up since then and, you know how it is, they wanted to thank us so they sent us two free tickets for tonight's show. I was gonna give 'em to Ed but, well, musta slipped my mind. They're yours if you want them."

Mr. Jarvin reached into his drawer and slid the two tickets across the desk.

"I'd go, but my wife, she's afraid of magic. Thinks she's going to vanish into a black hole or something," Mr. Jarvin said. "I should be so lucky."

Andre looked over the tickets. They looked like good seats. "So now I get all the perks, too?"

Mr. Jarvin got up from his chair and walked Andre to the door. "Enjoy," he said as Andre exited the office.

"Thanks, Mr. Jarvin. And don't worry about the article."

Mr. Jarvin patted Andre on the back. "Who's worried? I'm sure nothing but great things await."

IV

"All right, Apaches, come to order!"

The group of nine-year-old boys excitedly filling water balloons quickly calmed down and came to order just as their camp counselor had instructed them to do.

"Here's the plan," Shawn informed them with the zeal of a general about to take his troops into battle. "The Wonder Women will be here in a few minutes and we've got a little surprise for them, don't we?"

Some of the Apaches could barely contain their excitement and began to giggle.

"Now, pay attention, men. When I yell 'Geronimo!' that's when we pull out the water balloons and pound them. Until then, try to keep them hidden and act cool," Shawn told his troops.

"Yeah, cool," one of the Apache boys repeated, and they all nodded.

"But there is one rule," Shawn said with a sudden seriousness that got all of their attention. "Nobody is allowed to hit their chief. Nobody! Does everyone understand that? Hitting the chief with a water balloon is off-limits."

All the Apaches bobbed their heads up and down.

"I said, 'Does everyone understand that?'" Shawn repeated with an extra burst of energy.

"YES!" shouted his campers at the top of their lungs.

"Now that's more like it," Shawn said. "Gwen, the tall one, she's their chief, and she's the one who is to stay dry. Everyone else is fair game, but if I catch even one of you throwing a water balloon at her, I'll . . ." Here Shawn made a very disturbing screech. "I'll skin you alive, like the old Apache chiefs used to do. Got it?"

The boys again bobbed their heads up and down with a tinge of fear in their eyes. Shawn looked out onto the horizon.

"All right, then, here they come. Get ready, Apaches."

The Apaches stood up, milled around, and tried to act inconspicuous. A pack of nine-year-old girls approached from the other side of the park. As anyone could see by the way they marched in orderly fashion behind their leader, Gwen, a tall, pretty Latina with olive skin and a summertime tan, the Wonder Women were a dignified crew.

At the other end of the park, Andre pulled into the parking lot, got out of his car, and started walking toward Shawn.

Like a troop of soldiers, the fifteen or so Wonder Women came to a halt when Gwen held up her hand. She formally addressed the Apaches with a straight spine. There was pride in her voice.

"We, the Wonder Women, would like to present the chief of the Apache men a special token of our friendship before the weekend begins. If your leader would please step forth and kneel."

Shawn turned around and winked to his group. They giggled with the anticipation of having a secret the Wonder Women didn't know about. Shawn stepped forward with a smile on his face.

"Now, close your eyes," Gwen instructed, "and hold out your hands."

Shawn cast another sly look at his troops and did as he was told.

"All right, Cindy, give it to him," Gwen commanded. With that, Cindy, an adorable nine-year-old wearing a Camp Biddy Buddy T-shirt, walked up to Shawn.

Andre made his way closer, watching the scene

with a smile on his face. This was indeed, he thought, the perfect job for Shawn.

"O chief of the Apaches! We give you this," Cindy said as she reached into her bag. Shawn, playing along, kept his hands out and his eyes closed.

Suddenly, Cindy pulled out a water balloon and blasted it over Shawn's head. The shock of the cold water startled him, and, before he knew it, the entire troop of nine-year-old girls was pounding him with water balloons.

"Geronimo! Geronimo!" Shawn yelled at the top of his lungs.

Instantly, a water-balloon war broke out, with boys slamming girls and girls slamming boys and everyone running around trying to smash and soak everyone else.

"Get their leader! Get their leader!" Shawn yelled, but in the midst of the commotion, his instructions went unheeded. All that the Apaches remembered was *not* to hit the girls' leader, and no matter how much Shawn screamed, no one was about to violate his original orders at the risk of being skinned alive.

"Attack their chief! Attack their leader!" Shawn yelled, but none of his boys listened. Gwen laughed her head off.

"I can't believe it," Shawn said in dismay as he looked at his soaked T-shirt.

"Believe it," giggled Gwen.

"Well, looks like you're having fun," Andre said as he walked up to the two chiefs.

"Just another day at the office," Shawn replied as he realized that his sneakers were wet, too. "Damn!" he said with a squish. Gwen continued to giggle the type of giggle that could melt a man's heart if he listened to it for too long.

"Andre, I would like you to meet Gwen, the girl who just double-crossed me." Shawn imitated the high-pitched tone of a girl's voice. "'You make sure they don't hit me and I'll make sure they don't hit you.'"

Gwen laughed some more.

"Man, what a sucker I am," Shawn said as he assessed the damage.

Gwen offered her hand to Andre. "Hi. Nice to meet you," she said with a confident shake.

"The pleasure's all mine," Andre replied. "Any girl who can get the better of this guy is my instant friend."

Shawn wiped some water off his face and wrung out the hem of his wet shirt. "So what brings you down here? Reconsider my little offer, did ya?"

Suddenly Tammy, a gorgeous blond counselor, ran up to the three of them and interrupted as if a hospital were on fire.

"Shawn, Shawn, I must— Oh, hi," Tammy said to Andre and Gwen as an aside. "I must, like, totally speak to you, like, right now."

"Okay, okay, don't have a giraffe," Shawn said. "Shoot."

"Not here," Tammy said, as if the thought of this conversation taking place in the open were completely ridiculous. "It's, like, totally private."

Shawn flashed a devilish smile to Gwen and Andre. "Of course, my dear. Step into my office."

Shawn's office, of course, was nothing more than a patch of grass just a few yards away by a tree in the middle of the park. He escorted Tammy there, leaving Gwen and Andre alone with dozens of kids going bonkers in the background.

Gwen watched Tammy fawn over Shawn, her nonverbal signals saying more than her words ever could have. "They just can't keep away from him, can they?" Gwen said to Andre.

"Who, Shawn? Yeah, he's always been too cute for his own good," he replied as they watched Shawn raise Tammy's hand to his mouth and chivalrously kiss her ring. "He's just so adorable, isn't he?"

"You sound as if you have known him for a long time," Gwen said.

"Yeah, forever. We used to be on the same Little League team. In practice, I would pitch to him and strike him out and then he would pitch to me and whack me in the head. Even back then he was a wild man."

Shawn swept Tammy into a ballroom dance across the grass.

"I guess he hasn't changed that much, huh?" inquired Gwen.

"Nope, not much at all," replied Andre. "He tried to convince me to become a counselor this summer but, well, you know."

"Why didn't you?" Gwen asked.

"Oh, I got this job at *Affairs* magazine and I really couldn't pass up the opportunity. You know, the future, that type of thing," Andre said as an Apache boy ran past with a water balloon cocked and ready to fire at an unarmed girl. "But I must say, it looks kind of fun around here."

"I know that magazine," Gwen said. "You didn't write that piece on killer bees, did you? What great imagery. That was scary."

"No, wasn't me," Andre answered.

The same boy who was chasing the girl two

seconds earlier was now being chased himself, hunted down by three Wonder Women who were armed to the teeth and seeking to destroy him.

"What about that article on childhood education through fairy tales?" Gwen asked. "I mean, I agreed with some points. After all, fairy tales are a part of childhood, but if you take a moment to analyze the stereotypes they perpetuate you have to admit that some serious questions are raised."

"Well, uh, yeah but no, sorry, wasn't me," Andre replied.

"Okay, what about that piece on magicians? *Qué fantástico!* I loved that article. I mean, how amazing to learn about all the training and dedication a magician goes through. What they do really is an art. And some of those tricks!" Gwen said with a genuine enthusiasm. "I mean ever since I was a kid, I just——"

"Sorry, not me either," Andre admitted, looking down at his shoes. "I mean, I'm not really a writer yet. I mean, I am, but not an official one, you know? Well, that's not true either, 'cause I just got my first assignment, but, well, we'll see how it works out."

"I'm sorry. I didn't mean to—— It's just that when you said you worked for a magazine, I assumed you were a writer because you just kinda look like a writer, you know?" Andre's heart jumped out of his chest when he heard that. "I don't mean that in a bad way, though. I'm not talking about one of those writers who hasn't showered for a month and has groceries delivered to him through the mail slot. I just thought that maybe you might, you know, be one because, well, you know, my father has a subscription to *Affairs* and you can never underestimate the power of coincidence."

"The power of coincidence?" Andre repeated.

"Yeah, *coincidencia*—the power of coincidence," she replied. "You do believe in the theory that there is no such thing as a mere coincidence, don't you?"

"Of course, of course. I'm a huge fan of *co-in-see-dents-see-aah*," Andre replied. "Or there not being any such thing as one. A huge fan." Just because Andre wasn't exactly sure what the heck Gwen was talking about was no reason to break the flow of this conversation, he thought. Not when Gwen had a body like that, it wasn't.

"Well, isn't that a coincidence?" said Gwen with a soft smile. There was a pause. Andre and Gwen looked at each other. Her eyes were the color of coffee with caramel.

"Hey, sorry about that," Shawn said as he marched back over.

"That's okay," they both said at the same time, looking away from one another.

"But you know how it is when you are as popu-lar as I am," Shawn added, puffing out his chest.

"Yeah, we know," replied Andre.

The three of them looked out into the park and saw total chaos. There wasn't a dry camper any-where and dozens of water balloons were still zinging back and forth.

"Well, I guess it's about time we gathered up the little monsters and sent them home for the weekend," said Gwen. "Hey, Jenny!" she shouted. "Let go of that boy's nose!"

"Yes, I agree. We Apaches have thrashed you long enough and now the battle must end," Shawn replied. "Hey, tell those girls to stop stepping on his face. Run, Jason! Run!" shouted Shawn.

Gwen turned to Andre. "Well, it was real nice to meet you. Maybe we'll catch you around again some-time?"

"Sure, oh, by all means," answered Andre. "It was nice meeting you, too."

Gwen waved good-bye and headed off to start gathering up her campers.

"I'll meet up with ya in a sec, Gwen," Shawn said as he turned and started walking Andre back toward the parking lot. "So, what brings you down here today? Looking for a mean game of kickball?"

"Huh? Oh, I um, wanted to tell you, I got some free . . ." Andre, absentminded, wasn't really paying attention. He stopped and turned around. "Stay here a second, would ya?"

"What? Where are you going?"

Andre broke into a jog. "Gwen. Gwen, wait up a minute."

"Sure, what's up, Andre?"

He paused, unsure of where to start. "You see, I have these, well, my boss kind of gave me . . . Let me start again." Andre took a deep breath. "I have two tickets to a magic show tonight and I was thinking that since you said you liked magic that, you know, maybe you would want to go. . . ." He sort of stammered. "With me?"

Gwen scanned Andre for a moment and paused. Who knows what a woman thinks when she assesses the information gathered from this type of data collection? For Andre, as for most males, it was one of those five-second moments that felt like five years.

"Sure," she replied with a smile.

Andre looked up. Her eyes were sparkling. "Really? I mean, great."

"Yeah, really, I'd love to go," she answered. "I mean, if that is what you were asking me."

"Oh, no, yes, of course that's what I am asking

you. Great. Okay. Um." Andre took a pen out of his pocket (one of the benefits of being a writer was that he always had a pen) and gave it to Gwen so she could scribble down her phone number. "The show is at seven-thirty, so . . ."

"Pick me up at six?" she asked.

"Sure. Six o'clock works perfectly," Andre said as he put her phone number into the safest part of his pocket.

The two of them stood there looking at each other, not quite sure how to say good-bye. "Well, I guess I'll see you later."

"*¡Hasta luego!*" she replied with a perfect accent.

"Bye," Andre said as he floated back toward where he had been chatting with Shawn. Gwen turned to gather her monsters.

"Well . . ." Shawn asked, with his arms crossed, when Andre finally touched down.

"Well what?" Andre asked, trying to act cool.

"Well, wassup wit' that?" Shawn asked again.

"Wit' wut?"

"Oh, don't give me that. What's up with you making the little play right there?" Shawn said, wiggling his hips like a hula girl from the Hawaiian Islands.

"It's nothin', all right? I just think, you know,

she's cool, and we're going to go out tonight," Andre answered.

"You do-o-o-g!" Shawn fired back. "*Woof! Woof!* Dogman in the house. *Woof! Woof!*" When Shawn started to bark Andre knew it was time to leave. With a smile on his face and a phone number in his pocket, he departed.

"Later!" he called out as he floated off toward his car.

"Hey!" called Shawn as he jogged back up to Andre, not letting him get off that easily. "Why'd you come all the way down here anyway? You get fired?"

"I did not get fired," Andre replied with a wave of his hand.

"You get sexually harassed? I bet it was that skinny girl with the mustache. I knew she was gonna make a play for you once she let her sideburns grow in."

"Look, Mr. Apache, if you want to know the truth," Andre replied, "my boss gave me two tickets to tonight's magic show at the Forum Club."

"Awesome, I love magic," Shawn said with an excited smile.

"So does Gwen," Andre said. Shawn's smile disappeared. "Aw, you know how it is, buddy. You gotta do what you gotta do, right?" Andre said, trying to brighten the spirits of his friend. "It's like I always say, Shawn, never underestimate the power of *co-in-see-dents-see-aah*."

"What? You never say that," Shawn replied.

"I do now," Andre smugly said as he made his way to his car.

"I gotta say, dude, Gwen is a hottie," Shawn added as he watched her wrangling the campers. "I woulda made a play for her myself, but you know how those Latin ladies get if they find out you're trying to juggle females on 'em. That salsa in their blood gets mighty fiery, if ya know what I mean. Hey, you gonna try to—"

Andre cut him off before he could get nasty. "Don't you have some kids who need a role model or something? Get back to work."

"Tomorrow's Saturday. See ya on the court, right?" Shawn called to him as he headed in the other direction.

"Your lesson is at ten-thirty," Andre answered. "Don't be late."

"We'll see who gives who a lesson," Shawn said as he turned around and started jogging back to his campers. "Hey, Jimmy, come here, you little traitor."

Andre watched Shawn grab little Jimmy, flip him upside down, and spin him in a circle by the ankles as if he were a human rag doll. As blood rushed to Jimmy's head a huge grin spread across his face. Andre shook his head, smiled, and put the key in the ignition of his car.

V

Poof! A cloud of smoke rose from the stage as a magician in a black tuxedo made a white dove appear from underneath his cape. Gwen and Andre, sitting in prime seats right in the front row, looked on, amazed. The magician gently set the dove down in Gwen's hand. Her smile was radiant.

So was Andre's, but not because he was looking at the bird.

The evening passed with the sweetness of a pleasant dream.

After the show, Andre and Gwen sat inside Andre's car just in front of Gwen's house. The motor was off. Although they had been talking nonstop for hours, the past three minutes had been filled with more silence than words.

"Well, thanks again for taking me to the show. I had a really great time," Gwen said to break the stillness.

"Me, too. Those guys are amazing, huh?" Andre responded, keeping the conversation going.

"Absolutely," Gwen answered. "That last magician was incredible."

They both smiled again and stopped talking. There was another moment of awkward silence. Andre toyed with the steering wheel. Gwen fidgeted with her hair.

"Well, thanks again for the show," Gwen said.

"Yeah, it was a lot of fun," Andre answered.

"Well, I guess—"

Andre interrupted her, bolstered by a moment of courage. "Do you want to go out aga—"

"Yes," she answered before he had a chance to finish the sentence. "I mean, *por su puesto*, of course." They both giggled. "I'll give you a call and tell you when is good."

"Great," said Andre.

"Great," said Gwen.

Andre tried to think of something else to say, something clever and witty.

"Yeah, great," he said again. For a writer, that was a pretty disappointing effort.

"Well, good night," Gwen said as she moved to exit the car.

Andre hurriedly got out and ran around to open the door for her. When Gwen had stepped out of the vehicle they stood face-to-face. Andre looked as if he were about to kiss her.

"Well, good night," Gwen said in a soft voice.

"Yeah, good night," Andre answered.

There was another pause. Andre almost leaned in for a kiss. He debated it, thought about it, mulled it over, deliberated about it, and tossed it back and forth over and over again. Should I lean in for a kiss? he asked himself. He weighed the issue so much, so thoroughly, for so long, that the opportunity passed him right by. Gwen turned and started walking toward her house.

Damn! he thought.

Eyes down, Andre slowly started the long walk back around the car to the driver's-side door. I'm such an idiot, Andre thought.

Suddenly Gwen called out to him. "*¡Espera!* Wait. I don't have your phone number."

"Oh, you're right," Andre said as he took out a pen and scribbled down his number for her. He handed her the piece of paper and their hands touched. Neither pulled away. Andre looked at their hands and then looked into Gwen's eyes. He leaned forward and gave her a soft, gentle kiss. It was sweet, as first kisses are supposed to be. Time seemed to stand still.

When their lips parted, both Andre and Gwen smiled. Gwen put Andre's phone number into her purse, ran her fingers through her hair, and made her way to the door, then slipped inside the house.

Andre started the car with the taste of Gwen's lipstick still on his tongue. He put the blue Honda in gear with a smile, turned on the headlights, and started the sweet drive home.

That night when the clock read 3:18 A.M. it might as well have said high noon, because Andre was wide awake, typing away at the computer as if it were the middle of the day and the sun were shining. In fact, the sun was shining. It was shining inside his heart.

Andre's whole evening had been perfect. Things, of course, would have been drastically different had he heard the bearded guy in the back of the club get a big laugh from his buddies when he said, "Why oh why is a honeypot like that sitting with a nigger?"

But Andre hadn't heard, and his evening was bliss.

VI

"Man, I couldn't keep that chick off me last night."

"I'm crying for ya," said the long-limbed Lorenzo as he dribbled the ball before going off the bank from about twelve feet out.

"Yeah, well, you should be," Shawn answered. "I don't even know if I'll have the legs to play at full strength today." The guys were loosening up, taking a couple of jumpers and stretching their hamstrings before the game. "I tell ya, it ain't easy being in demand by all these beautiful women."

Andre nailed a jump shot. "I'm sure it isn't."

"So, how'd you do last night?" Shawn asked as he fed Andre the ball for another jumper. *SWISH!*

"I had a good time."

Shawn kicked the ball out to Andre again. "Had a good time? What the heck does that mean?" he asked as Andre drained yet another jumper from about eighteen feet away. "Did you have a good time or did you have a 'good' time?"

SWISH! "I had a good time, all right?"

This time, instead of just kicking the ball out to Andre, Shawn stepped in front of him to play a little defense. "How good?" he asked.

"Is that all you think about?" Andre responded as he started backing Shawn down with his back to the basket. "I went out with a girl who is smart and interesting and fun. Qualities the girls you go out with are very short on."

"Okay, okay, don't get all bikini-waxed on me," Shawn said as he muscled up to Andre. "But I'll let you in on a little secret, buddy. The girls I go out with are fun. They're very 'fun,' if you know what I'm saying."

As Shawn laughed at his little joke Andre took advantage and gave him a small head fake to the right, went left, and kissed the ball off the backboard for an easy left-handed layup.

"I gave you that," Shawn said.

"Man, get outta here," Andre answered.

There were nine players on the court, including Andre and Shawn, all of whom kept taking warm-up shots. Everyone was good to go, ready for a game, but were still waiting on something before they began.

Rolfie, a lean hoopster from the hood, approached Andre. "Yo, where's that crazy cousin of yours, Andre? I thought we were gonna play some ball today."

"Yeah, where is that fool?" Shawn added. "You think Cedric's too nervous about tonight to come out and shoot the rock around?"

"I don't know where he is," Andre replied, taking off his Hoopster sweatshirt and putting it on the bench along the chain-link fence. "You're coming with me, though, tonight, aren't you, Shawn?"

"Me, miss this?" Shawn replied. "Not for nothin'. Ced is finally going to be doing something he is good at—being a joker."

Suddenly there was a loud *honk! honk!* in the distance. Everyone turned their heads. It was Cedric, honking his bicycle horn to announce his arrival in the grandest of fashions.

Cedric rode up on his lime-green junker, sporting a porkpie hat and high-top sneakers that didn't match. For extra excitement he tried to pop a wheelie on his junker, but the front handlebars got away from him and he had to bail out just before the big crash that was his landing. A cloud of dusty bits of straw from the basket flew up when the bike slammed against the asphalt, but Cedric managed to regain his balance without falling, and landed on his two feet. There was a second there, though, when everyone thought he might just land on his head. But much to everyone's chagrin, he didn't.

"Da-dummm!" he said with a bow as the bike lay there like a casualty of war. "Sorry I'm late, boys, I had to wash my ride. Gimme the globe!"

Cedric grabbed the basketball out of Lorenzo's hands and threw up a crazy hook shot from thirty-four feet away that bounced off the top of the back-board with a loud thump. "Damn. Well, maybe during the game. I'm loose—let's play." Everyone looked at him in astonishment.

"You fellas pick teams yet or have you been waiting for the Court Jester?" Cedric asked with an extra zing. "That's my stage name, you know. You guys are still coming tonight to watch me win those five hundred buck-a-rooskies, ain't you?" he asked Andre and Shawn.

"Yeah, we'll be there, Mister Jester," Andre answered.

"Good, then let's play some ball." Cedric grabbed the basketball. "Yo, Pauley, you runnin' with me?"

"Naw," Pauley answered.

"Then I'm scorin' on your freckled face first. Let's go. Ball's in. Check it up," Cedric barked.

Shawn looked at Andre and they both shook

their heads as the teams got ready to play. "Yep, he's real nervous," Shawn said as he jogged down-court to set up the offense.

Thump.

"Come on, Cedric, pass the damned ball!"

Andre's house was clean and comfortable, and it smelled like the good food that was always being cooked in its kitchen.

"Gimme a triple king!" yelled Teddy to Tina. Andre's younger brother, Teddy, was nine and his younger sister, Tina, was six, so triple kings for Teddy were not so uncommon when he was playing checkers against her in the living room.

"And make it tall!" Teddy ordered. He liked to rub it in.

Pops, Andre's slightly gray-haired father, relaxed in "his" chair with his feet up. It was the kind of chair every father ought to have, big and brown, with a butt-cheek mold indented in it from many years of use. This chair knew how to cushion Pops's rear end better than any other chair on the face of this earth, and, when he was home, he was the only one allowed to sit in it. Of course, when he wasn't home, Pops liked to believe that all of his kids respected his personal space and avoided his chair at all costs. But in truth, Pops's chair saw just as much, if not more, abuse, than any other piece of furniture in the house. Juice boxes had been spilled on it, macaroni-and-cheese had been dripped on it, and there were pepperoni pizza crumbs buried inside it. Maybe Pops did know about what really went on in his chair when he wasn't there, but, even if he did, he for damned sure didn't want to give up the illusion that there was still one last sanctuary of peace for him under the roof of his own home.

"Ahhh," he said as he relaxed into his chair and raised the volume on the TV with the remote control. "That's what I'm talkin' about."

Pops especially loved to watch television from his chair, particularly if there was some basketball on the tube, and on this night there was. He had chips, a soda pop, some ice cream in the freezer for the fourth quarter and, of course, the game. Everything was perfect. Everything except that his chair was too close to the living-room telephone. This was not a small problem, either, because on the telephone was where his oldest daughter practically lived.

If people got paid for yapping on the telephone, Theresa May Anderson would be a fifteen-year-old millionairess. Wow, could she yap. Day or night. To boy, girl, animal, or vegetable. Round the corner or long distance. If there was some yapping on the phone to be done, Theresa could do it. The only people it seemed she didn't yap with, on the phone or otherwise, were her family members. Other than that, if a person wanted to talk, Theresa was happy to talk back.

Pops swore to himself that one day he was going to figure out a way to stop all the phone yapping. Unfortunately, he knew in his heart that no matter what he did, no matter how cunning he thought he was, a teenage girl had the resourcefulness to whip his ass in a war of wills if he dared to call her out to battle. So Pops did what all good fathers do: he did nothing except bark empty threats now and then.

"I swear, I'm gonna cancel that phone one day!" Pops shouted as he turned up the volume on the television. "And a good day it will be indeed."

"Sshhh, Pops, I'm talking with Jayla," Theresa answered. "She thinks Rickee likes Taneesha, so can you please turn down the TV?"

Pops's one small measure of revenge was that he was hard of hearing in his right ear. That meant he always had to turn up the volume of the television a bit, extra loud, whenever he was in his favorite chair. A loud television, Pops discovered, could be like mosquito repellent to teenage girls on the phone. It just always seemed to drive the annoying little critters away.

"I'm sorry," Pops responded as he turned up the sound, by remote, even louder. "You say something?"

Theresa *har-rumph*ed and tried to turn her back, but the two adversaries kept disturbing each other. The whole phone war could have ended two years before if Pops had simply allowed Theresa to get her own phone line in her room. But when she suggested the idea, "It ain't proper and I'm not paying for it," was Pops's response. At the time, the decision made sense. Theresa was only eleven and too much phone time would have cut into her homework time. But now she was thirteen, and Pops hadn't seen her crack a book in ages. While that may have seemed an even better reason for Pops to continue to hold out, it in fact just eroded his resolve that much more, because he had that much less reason to torture himself over the whole matter. No matter what he said, she claimed she had already done her homework, and no matter what he did, she always was yapping on the phone. At this point in their relationship, Pops was on the verge of giving in, Theresa was building momentum (the whole family knew it), and chances were, Theresa's fourteenth-birthday present was already a done deal. The only question was, would

Pops's spirit be broken badly enough for him to get her a cell phone, or only a landline.

The doorbell rang. Nobody made a move. Whether Pops didn't budge because he didn't hear it or because he knew it wasn't for him anyway was something that only he could know. Theresa didn't budge because, well, that was Theresa.

The doorbell rang again.

"Doorbell," Andre said with an edge in his voice as he came out of his bedroom buttoning his shirt.

"Oh, was it?" Pops answered innocently.

"Yes," Andre said to Pops as he crossed to the front door. "And Heaven forbid you get it," he added as he passed Theresa. She just turned her back to him and kept on yapping.

For this particular visitor, though, nobody really needed to get the door anyway. "Wassup, Anderson family?" Shawn asked as he let himself in before Andre arrived to greet him. Why Shawn bothered to ring the doorbell at all anymore was a topic the Andersons had discussed many times over the years.

"You ready yet?" he asked Andre.

"Give me two minutes," Andre replied as he headed back into the bedroom.

Shawn walked over to little Teddy and Tina, gave each of them a high five, and then jumped one of

Teddy's kings for Tina, who hadn't seen the possible move. Teddy frowned, but Tina smiled.

"I'm still gonna whup you," Teddy told her when Shawn walked away.

Shawn waved a vague hello to Theresa, who may or may not have waved back, depending on whom you asked—not that Shawn really cared. He then strolled into the kitchen where Mrs. Anderson, Andre's mother, was working her magic, and gave her a big kiss on the cheek.

"Hiya, Shawn, baby. Did ya get any dinner yet?" Mrs. Anderson asked with a smile. "We got plenty of good stuff. Let me fix ya a plate."

"I don't know, Mrs. A., Andre and I are leaving in a minute or so," Shawn said as he poked around and took a look at what was on the counter.

"Aw, just a quick little something," Mrs. Anderson offered. "You want some taters and pot roast?"

"Really, I don't want to be any trouble," Shawn said as his mouth watered.

"Aw, it's no trouble, baby. Just say when." Mrs. Anderson started to load up a plate of food for him.

"Well, if you insist," Shawn answered, trying not to seem rude.

"More?" she asked.

"Yeah, sure, that sounds nice. I'll have one more biscuit, some extra gravy, a sweet potato and . . . and another slice of roast, no, two more slices of roast, please," Shawn said as Mrs. Anderson piled more food on the plate. "Yeah, that's good. More gravy, too. Yeah, great. Thank you!"

"Dude, we are leaving in three minutes!" Andre snapped as he saw Shawn's plate piled as high as the ceiling. Shawn almost jumped out of his skin and ducked behind Andre's mother for protection. "Why do you feed him, Mom? Shawn, don't you have your own kitchen?"

"Oh, let him eat, Andre. The boy needs his energy," chided Mrs. Anderson.

"Mmyeeah, energy," Shawn answered with a stuffed mouth from behind Mrs. Anderson.

"Two minutes," Andre said as he exited to go put on his shoes.

"He don't know how good he's got it, Mrs. A.," Shawn said. "My mom served me fried bicycle tires tonight."

"Aw, stop," Mrs. Anderson smiled.

"With grilled telephone cords on the side."

Mrs. Anderson dismissed him with a wave of her dish towel.

"I'm-a go say hello to Pops," Shawn said as he

exited the kitchen with his plate. "Thanks again for the grub."

"You're welcome, baby," Mrs. Anderson replied.

"Just let me know if you need some help cleaning up," Shawn added.

"Now, who you lying to, Shawn Vincent?"

"Oh, not me. I'd send Andre back in here before we left."

"Aw, scoot your tail on outta this kitchen. Go on," Mrs. Anderson ordered as she pushed Shawn into the living room.

"Hey, Pops," Shawn said as he entered. When Pops didn't respond, Shawn tried again, the next time with a bit more volume. "Hey, Pops!" Shawn hollered as he plunked another forkful of food into his mouth.

"Oh, hey, Sha— Damn, son, don't your mother feed you?" said Pops, noticing the size of the plate of food in Shawn's hand.

"She served me up some coat buttons from the barbecue," Shawn answered as he stuffed a huge bite of food into his mouth and gulped it down without chewing, as only a teenage boy can. Pops could only shake his head. "I'm like the white son you never had, huh?" Shawn asked.

"And never wanted, neither," Pops responded as he turned back toward the TV. Shawn grabbed a seat on the coach and continued to eat. "So, how's everything?" Pops asked.

"Can't complain," answered Shawn.

"Good, 'cause there's too many people complaining anyway. Everywhere you look, there's people drummin' up a ruckus," said Pops as he pointed to the television. "Always making a ruckus. Like aspirin for the headaches they cause don't cost a man money. Just take a look at this."

Pops turned the volume up even louder so that Shawn could better hear the television. This, of course, was completely unnecessary, because the volume was already too loud for anybody with normal hearing. As Andre walked into the room, dressed and ready to go, Pops pointed to the screen, where a story on the news was playing out.

"A provocative demonstration by the PPA—People for a Pure America—will go on right here tomorrow as scheduled despite the many protests against this exhibition," the lady newshound for channel nine said to the camera. "The overwhelming sense of disapproval by many of our city's residents also means that the police will be out in full force because, as we know only too well, where there's hate, there's violence. This is Paula Plane, Action Nine News."

The television cut from a shot of a white

supremacist to pictures of police trying to quell a mob with batons. Fires burned in the background. Despite the fact that these were past events that had occurred years ago in places far away, local news always liked to keep the clips on hand and show them to spice up their current broadcasts.

Pops zapped the television, changing back to the basketball game. "It's a damned shame. A damned shame, I tell ya," he said.

"I have no desire to think about any of that stuff," Andre said as he stood up and smoothed out his shirt. "Come on, Shawn, let's get out of here and see if Cedric can make us laugh." Andre called out, "Good night, Mom."

Mrs. Anderson stuck her head out of the kitchen. "You boys leaving? Shawn, baby, I've got some pie."

Shawn checked his watch and then looked at Andre with puppy-dog eyes. "Well, the show doesn't start till—"

Andre grabbed Shawn by the jacket and pulled him out the door. "No. We're going."

"Maybe later," Shawn called back.

"I'll leave a nice piece out."

"You got any whipped cream?"

"Better," Mrs. Anderson responded. "Ice cream."

"Awesome," Shawn exclaimed as Andre frowned. "I know where I am coming back to tonight. Thanks, Mrs. A."

"Now, stay out of trouble, boys," Mrs. Anderson reminded them.

"They said the trouble is going to be tomorrow," Pops answered, speaking to no one in particular.

"Bye, Pops," Andre said as he returned and kissed his father on the top of his head from behind the chair.

"Yeah, see ya, Pops," Shawn said as he, too, returned and kissed Pops on the top of the head. Pops quickly jumped out of his chair, but Shawn was too quick for him and made it back to the door.

"I'll whomp on you, boy!" Pops threatened. Shawn smiled and closed the door.

VII

As Andre and Shawn walked up to the door of the Cuckoo Clock Night Club a neon sign flashed, AMATEUR NIGHT—$500 CASH PRIZE. Unfortunately, neither of them understood just how amateur the night was going to be until they heard Preston Trager, the fifty-three-year-old, banjo-playing, harmonica-humming, one-man, rock 'n' roll extravaganza band, butchering the Sinatra classic "My Way."

As Preston hit the last note, a forty-something emcee, who looked as if he sold used cars during the day, came out on stage and tried to rally some applause.

"Give it up for Preston Trager. Preston Trager, ladies and gentleman," chimed the emcee.

Preston took a bow and exited the stage to a smidgen of applause.

"And now for our next act here at the Cuckoo Clock, won't you please welcome the amazing talents of expert ventriloquist Shirley Mackey and Sidekick Sam."

Although the crowd was of a pretty good size—the place was maybe three-quarters full—Preston Trager had hardly warmed up the audience for Shirley Mackey. As a matter of fact, in professional show-biz terms, the audience was best classified as "ice-cold."

"Hi, I'm Shirley Mackey, and this is my dummy friend, Sidekick Sam." Shirley and her friend both wore silver sparkle–covered red vests—on her, a very poor wardrobe choice.

"Hi, I'm Sidekick Sam, and this is my dummy friend, Shirley Mackey," Sidekick Sam answered in a high-pitched shrill as Shirley moved her mouth. Truth be told, on Sidekick Sam the silver sparkle–covered red vest didn't look so bad.

One lone laugh echoed from the back of the audience.

"Wait a minute, who are you calling a dummy?" Shirley replied to her sidekick.

"Oops," said Sidekick Sam as Shirley's lips moved once more. The lone laugh once again rose from the audience.

"That's not funny, dude. Don't laugh," Rolfie said.

"Ssshh," Shawn hissed as he fixed his eyes back on the stage. "I want to hear."

"It figures you'd laugh at her," said Lorenzo, who

was all pimped out, wearing a classic Dr. J jersey with a matching old-school Philadelphia 76ers hat.

"What? She's funny," replied Shawn.

Andre rose from his seat. "I'll be right back," he said.

"You cool, Andre?" Lorenzo asked, sensing a bit of apprehension in his friend.

"Yeah, I'm cool. Just a bit nervous for Ced. You know, sometimes he can be a bit much. But I'm cool. I'll be right back," he said, and started to walk away.

"I'll wait here," Shawn replied, without taking his eyes from the stage. "I love ventriloquists."

"Well, if you see one let me know," said Rolfie.

"Hush," Shawn said, clearly not getting the joke. "I'm trying to watch."

Andre climbed through the crowd and ducked behind the thick red curtain that screened the back-stage area. He spotted Cedric waiting in the wings. For a moment Andre was worried he might have trouble finding Cedric, but when he spotted a top hat, silver bow tie, blue shorts, and orange high-tops, he didn't need to see more. Who else could it be? he thought. But what caught Andre even more off guard was that his first impression of the outfit wasn't of how ridiculous it looked, but of how, despite its crazi-ness, Cedric looked kind of sharp.

"Yo, what's up?" Cedric said upon seeing Andre.

"Looking good, Ced," answered Andre as he greeted his cousin with that special up-over-and-around high five.

"Would you get a load of that?" Cedric said, nodding toward the stage. "Her lips are moving more than that piece of firewood's."

"You're next, Mr. Jester," the emcee said to Cedric in a low, cold tone. The difference between the emcee's bright stage voice and insensitive backstage growl made Andre even more sure that this guy was either an insurance salesman or a bad dentist by day.

"You nervous?" Andre asked. "You know, about getting up and speaking in front of a big crowd?"

"Not at all," Cedric responded without giving the question a second thought.

"I know I'd be."

"Look, if you got something to say, speaking in front of people is easy."

Andre didn't seem so convinced.

"Just watch and take a lesson, cuz. Who knows, maybe someday you'll have to speak in front of a large audience to, like, I don't know, tell a hundred fourth graders to drink their milk or something."

"All right, all right, I'm going back to my seat.

We're over there at the second table," Andre said as he started to walk away. "We'll be rooting for you."

"Yo, Andre," Cedric called, halting Andre in his tracks.

"Yeah?"

"I just wanted to say, you know, thanks. Thanks for showin', dude."

"Hey, what are cousins for?" Andre replied. "Besides, at least one person has to laugh." Shirley Mackey told another joke and again, one lone laugh trickled from the audience.

"I mean one person other than Shawn," Andre added. They both smiled. "Go get 'em, Ced."

Cedric and Andre gave each other another high five, then Cedric adjusted his top hat and straightened his bow tie.

"I am good to go!" he remarked aloud to no one in particular. But all eleven other talent-show contestants backstage heard him.

Andre went back to the table, where he found about eight other people (ballplayers and other friends) who had come to see the show.

"So my doctor says . . ." Shirley Mackey began.

"Take two kangaroos and call me in the morning!" Sidekick Sam said, finishing Shirley's sentence as well as their performance. Not even Shawn laughed at that last joke. Sadly, Shirley left the stage to little applause.

"Let's give it up one more time for Shirley Mackey. Shirley Mackey and Sammy Sidekick, great job. Great job," said the emcee through a bright white smile.

"And now," continued the emcee in a super-charged voice, "our final performer of the night. Ladies and gentleman, won't you please welcome the Court Jester, Cedric Anderson."

Andre's table broke into a wild round of applause that seemed to blow a fresh breeze of life through the whole club.

Cedric strutted onstage beaming with confidence. The emcee went to shake Cedric's hand, but Cedric didn't waste any time with the formalities and went straight for the microphone. He grabbed it like a veteran Vegas comic and looked slowly over the audience before beginning.

"Why are there so many goddamned seeds in a watermelon?"

A burst of laughter came from the audience. Not just Andre's table, but other folks, too, wondering, Who is this guy?

Cedric patiently waited before continuing.

"Why are mangoes only ripe for two months out of the year?"

Another wave of laughter came. Cedric's delivery was superb.

"See, these are the problems you face being a black man in America today. Forget unemployment. Forget double standards. I want to know why extra-crispy fried chicken costs more than regular crispy fried chicken. I want to know why the insides of my hands aren't the same color as the outsides of my hands. I want to know why the only instrument you'll ever see a brother play in the orchestra at a classical music concert is a broom."

Laughter was everywhere, and a look around the club revealed a livelier mood in the audience. Cedric was doing well.

"You see, I wonder about these things. When I was a little kid I used to ask my momma these types of questions. But I'd never get an answer. Nope, nothing. All she'd say was, 'I'll show your fanny why extra-crispy costs more,' and that was the end of the conversation. And, you see, when a black momma says something like that, she means it, too. She'll wallop yo' ass in a heartbeat. A black daddy will give ya a lickin', and it'll hurt and all, but it's more infrequent. You know, like when you rob your first liquor store.

But Momma . . . *Damn!* She would hit you just about every day."

The audience howled. They really liked Cedric. He was calm, cool, and collected, and he had great timing. It seemed that everyone in the club wore a smile. Everyone except Andre.

"Momma will hit you even on days you don't do nothing. My feeling is, a black woman does this to make up for the days she knows you did something that she never found out about. *Thwap!* 'Damn, what's that for, Momma?' 'You know what that's for. I may not, but you damned well do. And if you do it again, I'll give ya anotha!' *Thwap!*"

Cedric had a very animated and amusing *thwap!*

"See, African American women have this gene. It's like some sort of DNA passed down from tribe to tribe many generations ago. It's called the *thwap!* gene. White women, ya'll don't have this one. It's a black thing—like sucking on pig's feet or never shutting up in a movie theater. And man, I am telling you, a black woman will *thwap!* you so hard, it will make your brother cry."

As Cedric held the audience under his spell Andre became more and more uncomfortable, shifting back and forth, unable to sitting still. The look on his face showed that something was not right. He fidgeted and frowned. Shawn, though, sitting right next to Andre, didn't notice a thing.

As the show wore on Cedric grabbed his crotch, mugged like a thug, and impersonated a crack addict. Andre smiled less and less until, finally, there was no more humor for him at all.

"And what is with all the negative stereotyping of black people. I mean, take for example the idea that all black men have large penises. Oh, please, stop, you're so cruel. And we can make love all night? No, stop, that's enough. What? We're sexual monsters who love to hump from dusk to dawn? Enough! No more! I can't take it anymore. Whatever you do, please, don't call me a good athlete."

A white woman in the front row rolled with laughter. Cedric looked at her and shook his head.

"Yeah, she's laughing now, but when she goes home tonight this joke won't seem so damned funny then. Not when hubby's asleep by ten-thirty and his engine is spent for the next week. But hey, at least he's got a job, right? Anybody want to buy a car stereo? I'm taking orders based on what's in the parking lot right now. Thanks, ya'll. Peace out. Good night."

Cedric took a bow and the crowd exploded with applause. The emcee, obviously impressed, although grudgingly, met him at center stage.

"The Court Jester, ladies and gentleman— Cedric Anderson."

Cedric took a second bow, and as the cheers continued, Shawn leaned over to Andre. "Wow, I had no idea he was this good. Ced was excellent. He's definitely going to win."

Andre squirmed a bit and looked around. "Yeah, he probably will."

"Hey," said Shawn. "What's the matter with you?"

"Nothing," Andre grumpily said as he got up. "Nothing. I'll be back in a minute."

Backstage, people milled around Cedric, congratulating him and basking in his glow. Even the other talent contestants knew that Cedric was the best one there. Andre approached with a solemn look on his face.

"Well, whaddya think?" Cedric asked with a huge grin. "Was I good or was I good? Go on, you can tell me. I'll put my usual humility on hold for a minute."

"Yeah, I guess it's funny stuff," Andre said in a soft voice.

"You guess it's funny stuff? What? Weren't you listening?"

"I mean, yeah, you're funny, Cedric. Real funny. But why do you have to do that kind of stuff?" Andre asked.

"Huh?"

"I'm talking about all of that black, race, stereo-type crap. You don't need to do that kind of material."

Cedric made a motion to knock on Andre's forehead. "Hello? Is anybody in there? What's the matter with you? I was funny. I was damned funny. People were rolling out there."

Another person walked up and offered Cedric his congratulations. Cedric happily shook his hand.

"You see? I was good. Good!" Cedric added.

"Yeah, but you can be good without ridiculing black people, can't you?"

"Yo, yo, wait a minute, cuz. It's just jokes, man. Comedy. Funny stuff that people like and want to hear. Nobody gives a damn anymore about why the chicken crossed the road."

"Man, that's a BS, Uncle Tom answer and you know it," Andre shot back.

"Say what?" Cedric asked as he moved a step closer. All of a sudden the two found themselves standing nose-to-nose without a lot of love in the air.

In the background the emcee addressed the crowd. "And tonight's winner of the five-hundred-dollar grand prize is . . . you guessed it, the Court Jester, Cedric Anderson."

The crowd erupted with applause. Cedric and

Andre glared at each other. After a tense moment, Cedric cracked a cocky smile and brushed an imaginary piece of lint off Andre's shoulder.

"That ain't no BS, cuz. That's winnin', you dig?" Cedric turned and strode back onstage with his hands raised high in the air proudly to claim his reward. Andre watched from the side of the stage as Cedric was handed a check.

After kicking a plastic garbage can, Andre stormed out the back door.

VIII

Sweat poured out of Andre's body. Cedric was playing defense on him, and covering him pretty well, too, but he was bodying him up a bit all over the court. Andre didn't give a damn, though. He was taking it to the rim regardless. He dribbled left, cut back to the right, and then spun around for a left-handed running bank shot in the lane.

No good.

The other team quickly got the rebound and pushed it up-court for a three-on-one fast break and an easy score. Andre, bent over, hands at his knees and sucking for air, motioned for the ball, and got it. He took two dribbles and quickly launched a twenty-seven-foot jumper that clanked badly off the rim. Cedric got the rebound and took a dribble the other way with nothing but the single-minded intention of going coast-to-coast.

Andre rushed up from behind, but Cedric had a step on him and there was no way Andre could get there in time. But rather than concede an easy layup,

96

Andre slapped Cedric's forearm with a loud *smack*, causing the ball to go sailing out of bounds, purposely taking the hard foul instead of giving up the easy hoop.

"Foul! I got one right here on the man who can't laugh."

"What'd you say?" Andre asked, quickly turning back around.

"I said, I'm suffering internal bleeding 'cause you ain't got no funny bone."

"You're the one who's gonna be bleeding if you keep talking trash."

"Oh, I'm shaking, Jealous Boy," Cedric mocked. "I'm shakin' in my shoes."

"Jealous Boy? Man, you got it so wrong," Andre said.

"No, I'm dead-on. See, I'm not ashamed of who I am," Cedric fired back. "I'm not embarrassed to be black. That's why I can feel free to laugh and make jokes about it."

"Say what?" Andre shouted as he headed toward Cedric. Everyone on the court was at a standstill. The two of them moved closer, neither backing down.

"You heard me, you're jealous. You're jealous cause I'm gonna be rich, you're jealous cause I'm gonna be famous," Cedric boasted, with sweat glistening over his whole body. "And the only reason you don't like the jokes I tell is because you feel guilty laughing at them."

"You need to shut up 'cause you don't know what you're talking about."

"Oh, I don't, huh?" Cedric responded with a swagger. "Well, at least I ain't gonna spend the rest of my life licking some white man's ass so I can write some meaningless words in a magazine that no one reads anyway. Maybe one day you'll get a BMW, Andre, and a condo on the beach to go along with your nonblack girlfriend. Maybe then you won't feel so bad laughing at my stuff."

"Let me tell you something," Andre said as he moved so close the two were face-to-face. "You don't make jokes about black people. You make jokes about niggers."

"So what you saying?"

"I'm saying, so what's that make you?" replied Andre, pointing his finger at his cousin's chest for extra emphasis.

"You see a nigger around here, you slap him, ya hear," Cedric snapped back, his breath hot on Andre's face.

Bang! All of a sudden the tension burst and Andre threw an overhand left that cracked Cedric in the jaw. Cedric retaliated with a right hook that popped Andre in the eye, and before anyone could react the two had tackled each other and were brawling at center court.

The guys quickly rushed to pull them apart, but it took six ballplayers to separate the two cousins. It was as if they were trying to rip each other's head off.

"Let me go! Nobody calls me a wannabe white boy!"

"Who's he calling a nigger? I'll kill his ass!"

Shawn finally managed to get between the both of them. "Cool it! Knock it off! Both of you!"

After more yanking and pulling they finally managed to get Andre and Cedric separated. Andre, whose shirt was torn and who had a golf ball–size knot forming over his right eye, angrily broke free from the ballplayers who were holding him back. After Andre was loose Cedric also wrestled himself free, his lip cut and bloodied.

The two of them heaved and took deep, angry breaths, like enraged bulls fighting in a meadow. Cedric spat and checked for the source of the blood. Andre felt the lump forming on his head and checked for blood himself. Finally, Andre threw down his hands in disgust, scooped his keys off the bench, and stormed away.

IX

Andre burst into his house and slammed the front door behind him. Nobody was home except Pops, who was watching a Sunday boxing match on television. The TV's volume was so loud, it was if his father had a ringside seat. Pops liked to hear the crisp *pfft! pfft!* of the punches.

Andre tried to march past his father and into his bedroom without having to explain himself, but Pops, without looking up, sensed something was up.

"Ho-o-o-o-o-old it! Stop right there. What is going on?"

Jeez, how do parents always know? Andre thought as he slowly turned around. His T-shirt was torn, his eye was swollen, and there was a nasty scratch on his neck.

The announcer's voice rang out from the TV. "And the young man from the West Side of Los Angelll-*eeeezz*, California is out! KO'd in the seventh. What a fight. What a fight!"

"It looks more like Anderson was knocked out to me," Pops remarked.

Andre exploded. "This Anderson wasn't knocked out. If anything, the other Anderson would have been knocked out. I'd have put such a whoopin' on him if—"

"Whoa, wait a minute! Slow down. Slow down!" Pops interrupted. "What other Anderson?" Pops paused. "Who, Cedric? You been fightin' with your own cousin, boy?"

"Oh, he ain't seen nothin' yet. Well, till I catch up with that fool. I'm really gonna—"

"Sit down, Andre."

"I don't want to talk about it." Andre turned to leave.

"Boy, I said *sit down!*" Pops thundered.

Andre stopped, lowered his eyes, and slunk his way over to the couch. Pops reached for the remote to turn off the TV, but the lady reporter from Action Nine News suddenly appeared with an urgent interruption.

"This is Paula Plane from Action Nine News with a breaking story. As expected, the PPA—People for a Pure America—held their rally this afternoon and, as expected, there were a lot of angry citizens there to greet them. Police were on hand to try to ward off any trouble, but tensions were high and tempers were short."

The station began to roll footage of the troubled event.

"As PPA leader Hans Vogel took to the microphone, hundreds of angry protesters shouted their disapproval."

Hans Vogel appeared on screen. He was a thin thirty-eight-year-old man with light brown hair who, surprisingly, was the exact opposite of a fire-and-brimstone speaker. His tone was calm, his manner reserved, and not once did he raise his voice. It was the crowd, as he stood at the podium, that became more and more unruly.

"Unmoved by his opposition, Hans Vogel spoke at length about his views on the minorities in our country," the reporter said.

"Blacks have rights. Jews have rights. Hispanics have rights. Where are the whites' rights?"

A surging cry of approval went up from a portion of the crowd, but it was quickly met with a chorus of emphatic boos from the other side of the gathering.

"Is it that whites do not *have* rights?" Vogel asked.

"As Vogel's discourse echoed throughout the parking lot," the reporter continued, "the crowd became more and more infuriated. Finally, in a flash of rage, an angry African American man tried to rush the podium, but security quickly intercepted him. That is when the trouble began."

The footage of the violent confrontation was both disturbing and hypnotizing, much like watching a train wreck in slow motion. Punches were thrown. An old lady was knocked to the ground. People were swinging signs like baseball bats. Nothing less than a miniature riot had broken out in the parking lot of the Hometown Shopping Mall.

Then the police intervened.

"Violence spread like wildfire. Officers of the law were forced to use riot gear and tear gas to disperse the crowd. Our Action Nine team was on the scene to speak to a few of those who were there."

An elderly man, a white man in his early fifties, spoke into the microphone.

"It's a shame. The PPA was formed not to hurt but to protect the children of this country and to protect our God-given values. It should never have come to this."

A thirty-year-old black man in a green sweater with horn-rimmed eyeglasses appeared next.

"This is pure racism! We must battle these forces any way we can."

There was a quick cut to a middle-aged white lady. "I don't think it's right that my children should have to put themselves forty thousand dollars in debt to attend college when minorities get scholarships every day to help them pay for the cost of an education. Think about it. It's a lot of money."

A black teenager with his hat on backward popped his head onscreen.

"Yo, yo, yo, is this thing on? Yeah, I ain't nobody's slave and never will be! Can ya di-i-i-i-g?"

The reporter reappeared on the screen. "Afterward, I arranged to speak with Hans Vogel."

"The PPA is a simple, peaceful organization. We are not founded in hatred. We are not rooted in rage and ignorance. On the contrary, we believe in education." Hans Vogel spoke softly and sipped a cup of tea. "African Americans have their culture. Hispanics have their culture. Jews, Muslims, Asians have theirs, too. And we have ours. What makes me racist when I say such a thing?"

"Is violence a part of this culture?" the reporter asked.

"We do not preach violence," Hans continued with a small shake of his head. "What we do is, we encourage participation through separation."

"Participation through separation? Can you explain?" the reporter asked.

"Essentially, my organization, the PPA, consists

of hardworking, taxpaying citizens who want to hold on to what they have while they still have it. We have earned it, we know we have earned it, and we want to pass it along. I ask you," Hans said with a soft look into the camera, "am I so wrong to want the best for my children, too?"

The reporter didn't answer. Instead she used Hans Vogel's last question as a bridge to the next news segment. "Well, that's the story from down here. Stay tuned for weather and sports. This is Paula Plane reporting live, Action Nine News."

Pops zapped off the television.

Andre jumped to his feet. "That is such *crap*! I just want to . . . ooh, look at the way he's all smooth talking and gentle, like he's baking apple pies or something. I mean, come on, he's separating people by color! No matter how much BS logic he tries to apply, it's still racism. Damn, I hate them! I just hate them all."

"Stop talking about all this hate. You hate this. You hate that. There's too much hate in this world already, son."

"Are you telling me that if that guy, Hans Vogel, came over here right now you wouldn't want to just . . . just rip the voice box right out of his throat or something?" Andre asked. "I mean, come on, Pops, I know you're seeing right through that garbage."

"You're missing the point," Pops answered.

"No, answer the question," Andre snapped back. "And none of that philosophical, intellectual mumbo-jumbo talk either. Just a straight answer. Would you or would you not want to make that man hurt for the words he is preaching?"

Pops paused. He noticed the bloodstain from Andre's earlier fight on his shirt and saw the vessels in Andre's forehead pumping hard.

His pause continued. Pops thought again about how to frame his response. After all, Pops was old enough to understand that just because someone asked him a hot-tempered question didn't mean he had to return with a hot-tempered answer.

"I'll answer the question," Pops finally responded. "But I'll do it in my own way."

"Oh, here we go," said Andre, throwing up his hands as if he had just proven a point to both of them. "Time for a speech."

"That is right, here we go. There's a little story—"

"Oh, surprise, a story."

"Yes, a story about how I lost the hearing in my right ear," Pops continued.

Andre, short on patience, stood up and cut his father off.

"Excuse me, but what does falling off a tall

ladder, aside from the metaphorical value—which I have yet even to see—have a damned thing to do with a guy like Hans Vogel?"

"I didn't fall off no hot-damned ladder, Mr. Know-it-all! I just told you that so you . . . so . . ." The words trailed off. Pops didn't want to speak out of anger, but Andre's know-it-all-ness had gotten to be too much. "I . . . Now just sit down and I'll tell you what really happened. That's if you can hold your tongue for a dang minute and listen up."

Andre's eyes met his father's and for a moment they were both ashamed of how they were speaking to one another. Andre quietly took a seat. Pops softened his tone.

"See, I always told you that I never went to college and I was ashamed of that. But the truth is that I did go. I did go to college, Andre." Pops reclined in his chair and looked off into the distance. "Boy, I tell you, I was a good-lookin' young man back then." Pops raised his eyes to the ceiling and smiled with fondness at this glimpse back at memories he obviously hadn't thought about for years.

"Mind you that this is before I even met your mother. You see, I won this scholarship because of an essay I wrote on the idea of equality after the Civil War. My parents were so proud of me. Their son was going to be the first black man in the family to go to a university. You remember Nana and Papa?"

"Not really. I was kind of young when they passed," Andre answered.

"Oh, you woulda liked my parents. They were great peoples. Great peoples." Pops continued. "Anyway, imagine me, unpacking my bags in my new dorm room, planning on being a student, maybe even a big-time record executive one day. You see, you're not the only one in this family who likes music."

Andre smiled.

"I loved school. I used to sit in class and take notes and listen to what the professors said and just drink it up like their words were glasses of honey." Pops slapped his knee at the thought. "Of course, I was the only black student in class. There were other black students on campus, but almost all of them were athletes and they weren't really there to get an education as much as they were there to run or throw. Same still goes on, I guess," he added with a shake of his head. "Maybe not. That wouldn't be really fair to say. Anyway, I was at college to learn, 'cause I always knew that learnin' was the best way to make something of my life."

"Did being one of the only black students bother you?" asked Andre.

"Not really. I mean, I noticed it, but I was young and pretty much just happy to be there. Anyway, one Friday," Pops said, getting back to his story, "there was this freshman dance. Every school has them. It was going to be my very first college party. I figured I'd get all dressed up, put on my best duds, you know how it is?"

"Don't tell me you wore purple."

"Andre," Pops shot back with a stern look. "I look *might-tee* good in purple."

"Oh, no," Andre said with a smile as he envisioned his father all pimped out, thinking he looked smooth.

"Yessirreee, I was looking snazzy at the dance, make no mistake," Pops continued. "Lookin' snazzy, feelin' good. College was treating me just fine. Well, that certain time came when nature called and I had to go to the bathroom."

Andre leaned forward in the chair and listened a bit more closely.

"I walked in to, you know, use the facilities, and there were these three white kids who were mixing booze into their punch."

"In the bathroom?" Andre asked.

"Sure. Back then you could get in trouble for that sort of thing if anyone saw you," Pops answered.

"They see me and I see them and, so as not to act like anything is wrong, I stepped up to the urinal and started going about my business anyway. I thought I was kinda sending a message like, 'No sweat, guys. You want to drink, I'm cool.'"

"But they didn't take it that way?" Andre asked.

"Sshhh, you're interrupting," Pops responded. "So I, you know, unzip my fly, take out my wang, and start doing my business. And then the biggest of these guys sort of winked at his friends, thinking I didn't see him and walked up to the urinal next to mine."

"But you did see him," Andre said.

"I just said I saw him."

"Oh, sorry."

"Can I finish?" asked Pops.

"Go ahead, go ahead," Andre responded, sitting almost at the edge of the chair.

"Always interrupting," Pops said with a shake of his head. "So the music is playing from outside at the dance and I'm alone in here with these three white boys and the biggest one, bigger than me at least, makes that sort of 'watch this' eye contact with his drunken buddies by the sink. Next thing I know, the big white guy who is using the urinal next to me looks over and says, 'Hey, nice boots.'"

110

"He started talking about your . . . oops, sorry," Andre said catching himself interrupting. "Sorry."

"So he says to me 'Nice boots' and then he turns from the urinal and starts pissing on them."

"He started pissing on your feet?" Andre exclaimed.

"Right there on my shoes," Pops replied. "And then he said something like, 'Lookie there, coon boy, I just washed the dust off 'em for ya.'"

"I just stared at him, cold and defiant. He might have been bigger than me, but that never meant nothin' to me," Pops continued. "I could hear his friends laughing it up pretty big-time in the background, too. Then suddenly, this big white guy, musta had six inches on me, he turned to me, poked me in the chest and said, 'Why ain't you laughing?' I just stood there silent as a stone. Then he poked his finger in my chest and asked me again, 'I said, why ain't you laughing, coon boy?' *Bang!*" Pops shouted. "I drilled him in the stomach and he hunched over sucking for air. *Bang!* After going low I went high and busted him in the nose. You could hear the crack of the bone echo through the whole bathroom and blood from his face sprayed everywhere against the wall."

Pops was out of chair reenacting the two punches he had thrown to crumple the kid. *Bang!*

Bang! Andre smiled with all the pride a son could muster at hearing this triumphant tale from his father's youth.

"As quick as that, it was over," Pops said. The two friends of the white kid were frozen and horrified. I mean their buddy's face was just mangled. I shouted at them, 'Either of you two want to mess with a coon boy? Do ya?' I guess the gruesomeness of what they saw me do to their big friend really spooked 'em, because they were visibly scared and parted ways for me to walk out of the bathroom like I was Moses and they were the Red Sea," Pops continued.

"Did you sock them, too?" Andre asked.

"Now, why would I do that? I mean, I just looked down at my boots and saw them ruined with piss and then I saw this big, stupid, drunk white guy with his nose spread all over the bathroom floor and, well, I just felt disgusted. You know, I couldn't believe it. All I wanted to do was leave, so I started to walk away."

"Oh," Andre said, sort of understanding that this wasn't a videogame fight he was talking about but a real encounter his father had had once upon a time back in college.

"So I started walking to the bathroom door to leave, but when I grabbed the handle—*boom!*"

"What do you mean, *boom?*" Andre asked.

"Boom," Pops repeated with a far-off look in his eyes.

"What? Did the big guy get up?"

"Naw," replied Pops.

"So what do you mean, *boom*?" Andre asked, getting upset that his father was holding back the details.

"One of those skinny punks cracked me upside the head with the bottle of liquor."

"You mean he blindsided you?"

"Right upside my noggin," Andre's father answered with a sad shake of his head. "I vaguely remember some shouting as I lay there like, 'I got him for you, Billy Ray. I got him for ya good!' but the truth is, I never saw who hit me."

There was a pause while Andre digested the weight of the story.

"Wow," he said softly.

"All I know is that I woke up three days later in the school hospital with a turban wrapped around my melon and my brain pounding like a jackhammer. And I couldn't hear out of my right ear."

"Not a thing?" Andre asked.

Pops shook his head. "Doctor told me that it was just temporary and that my hearing would probably come back in a day or two. Twenty-four years later I still can't hear a damned thing."

Andre sat quietly on the couch, sadness filling his heart.

"Did they ever find those guys?" he asked.

"You mean the police? Naw, they were no help."

"Well, did you go after them?" Andre began looking for a bit of resolution. "I mean, what happened? Jeez, Pops! I woulda hunted them down. I mean I woulda——"

"Been angry? Enraged? Vengeful? I was," Pops responded. "I was all of that and more. I bought a gun."

A gun? That caught Andre off guard. Pops had always been strongly opposed to any kind of firearms.

"Did you use it?" Andre asked. This was a question to which he wasn't sure if he really wanted the answer. "Did you get revenge?"

"Revenge? How can someone really ever get revenge, Andre?" Pops said with a shake of his head. "It doesn't exist."

Pops looked at Andre in a soft, caring way. It was the kind of look only a person who has gone through a really bad experience can give to someone who is naive about such things. Andre, despite all his brains and achievements and experiences, was, after all, still a teenager. "Aw, you'll understand what I'm saying one day," Pops added. "Me, I learned the hard way."

"The hard way? How?" Andre inquired.

"I got busted, that's how," Pops replied. "See, what happened was, somebody saw a young black kid running around with a gun in his belt and called the cops. I was thrown in jail for four nights."

Pops stopped speaking as if that were the end of the story. Maybe for him it was, but for Andre there had to be more.

"So, what happened?" Andre asked.

"What do you mean, what happened? I sat in jail for four nights, that's what happened. What, you want details? I was thrown into a cell with criminals, real criminals, Andre. They stole my food and wouldn't let me use the toilet."

"They wouldn't let you use the toilet?" Andre gulped, frightened by the idea.

"I couldn't take a shit for four days," Pops responded, adding color to his commentary. "I was scared stiff and they knew it, too. It sure didn't take me long to realize that jail was not the place for me. Soon enough I made bail and got probation."

"So," Andre added after a pause to think it all over. "You never found those guys who hit you with the bottle, huh?"

"I stopped looking," Pops said with a resigned air. "Matter of fact, I stopped everything. I dropped out of school and didn't do squat for the next two and a half years. Did nothing at all but feel sorry for myself. Eventually, I went on, got a decent job, and married your mother."

"You did more than get a decent job, Pops," Andre affirmed. "You got lots of business going on."

"Yeah, I guess I did okay. I mean, I raised a family and paid my bills. But I still have regrets."

"About not finding those guys who hit you?" Andre asked.

"Naw, who cares about them? My regrets are about other things. About giving up. That's what I regret. I became a victim."

"But it wasn't your fault. You got hit in the head with a bottle just because you were black."

"No, Andre. I wasn't a victim when I got hit in the head with a bottle. I became a victim when I let my chance to go to college get away. I had it and I let it go," Pops said with regret in his voice. "I can blame this or I can blame that, but I had my dream right there in front of me and I let it get away. Hell, at the end of the day, it's nobody's fault but mine."

A tear started to form in his eye.

"There's too much hate in this world, Andre. Too much hate. And it does nobody no good."

Pops inhaled deeply, which somehow seemed to signal the end of his story.

Andre looked at his father with a mixture of sadness, sympathy, and admiration, and then looked at his Hoopster T-shirt. It was torn at the neck from the fight with Cedric. Andre lifted a piece of material to see if it could be sewn back together somehow, but after fiddling around with it for a moment he realized it couldn't. The shirt was ruined.

Pops rubbed his eyes and caught his breath. This was a story he'd never planned for Andre to hear, and yet, something inside him told him he had always known the day would come when he would have to tell his son the truth about how he had really lost the hearing in his right ear.

Andre rose from his seat, crossed over to his father, and gave him a hug.

"I love you, Pops," Andre whispered into his father's deaf ear.

"I love you too, Andre," Pops replied, hearing every word.

The digital clock flipped from 3:07 to 3:08 A.M. Not a bird chirped, nor did a car pass on the street. All was quiet.

Suddenly Andre threw the covers off, rose from the bed and switched on the light at his desk. After sitting down in the chair he removed three spiral notebooks from the top drawer, two of which were already filled with pages and pages of random writings. The third notebook was blank. Andre shuffled through his old notebooks, put them aside and opened up to the first virgin page of the new, untouched notebook. With a violent tear he ripped out the first page, crumpled it up, and tossed it in the wastepaper basket.

"For good luck," he said to himself. And then he began.

At the top of the page Andre wrote the following words:

MY BROTHERS

by

Andre Anderson

X

The pitch-black sky stretched silent and still, when a blast followed by an explosion of fireworks lit up the evening in an array of brilliant colors. White, silver, blue, red, and green dripped from the night above as if a paint can had been spilled in heaven. Children screamed as they swooshed through the loop of a roller coaster. Two young lovers walked side by side, sharing cotton candy and secrets. American flags, barbecue, blue jeans, and firecrackers bombarded the senses. It was the annual Fourth of July amusement-park party and, as always, the soccer stadium playing field was filled with folks from all around, spending money, eating food, riding rides, and laughing loudly.

Andre and Gwen walked hand in hand through the carnival like any one of a thousand other couples. They smiled, made silly jokes, and engaged in small talk that revealed much more about themselves than either one would ever have admitted.

"How old were you when you first kissed a girl?" Gwen asked Andre with a mischievous light in her eyes.

"Do grandmothers count?"

"No, real girls," Gwen said.

"But what if it was on the lips?" Andre asked.

"That's disgusting," Gwen replied, but she laughed anyway. "No, really. How old were you?" she persisted.

"I was thirteen. It was Eileen Wanesmoor by the old lake," Andre fessed up. "How about you?"

"I French-kissed Jimmy Sumpton by the pool. He had little stomach muscles. I was ten."

"You French-kissed a boy when you were only ten years old?" Andre asked in disbelief. "What a slut!"

"We were playing truth or dare," Gwen responded. "I didn't really know what I was doing. I kind of licked his tooth."

"That's gross," Andre said, turning away and walking a little faster. Gwen smiled, jogged up to him, and turned him back around to give him a nice, sweet kiss on the lips.

"Stop," Andre said, not wanting her to stop at all. "Who knows where that tongue has been?"

"*Oye, ven aquí,*" Gwen said, kissing him all over his face. "Let me brush your teeth for you."

"Yuck, no," Andre said with a huge smile.

"Step right up and win your honey a teddy! Step right up! Step right up!" a carnival barker called out.

Gwen and Andre had wandered down to the

basketball shooting game, where an attendant was trolling for business.

The sound of a bouncing basketball immediately caught Andre's ear. He looked over and saw a chubby, forty-five-year-old white guy badly miss a shot.

"Aw, too bad," said the attendant without a shred of sympathy in his voice. The attendant was male, about thirty, with sweaty hair, and he was chain-smoking cigarettes.

"Hold it. I'm going to win your heart with my jump shot," Andre said to Gwen as he eyed the basketball gallery.

"It's going to take more than a jump shot to win my heart," Gwen replied.

"All right, then I'll win you a teddy bear, which I'll use as an evil ploy to get into your heart," Andre said. "And maybe other places, too," he added with a mischievous grin.

Gwen flushed at Andre's words, never expecting to hear such innuendo coming from Andre's clean mouth. Then again, she was also a bit excited.

"You must be feeling a little lucky tonight," she replied.

"Yeah, I could be."

"Yeah, you could be," Gwen teasingly answered.

They both smiled. Andre led Gwen over to the basketball shooting gallery, where he took out some money from his pocket and slapped it down.

"Gimme three," Andre said. The attendant placed three balls in front of Andre. He picked them up and rapidly fired them off with his sweet, left-handed shot. One. Two. Three. *SWISH! SWISH! SWISH!*

"Which one do you want?" he asked, looking at the wall of stuffed animals.

She pointed at a giant panda with a big, black nose. "*¡Ésa!* I want that one!"

"Let me have that one," Andre said to the attendant, pointing to the panda that Gwen had pointed out.

"Oh no, friend. You can't have that one. Youse is gotta choose from dem over dere." The attendant pointed to a small row of junk in the back. There were key chains, brightly colored shoelaces, and a couple of two-inch-high stuffed animals. All of it looked like ninety-nine-cent-store trash.

Andre gazed back at the attendant. The attendant took a long drag off his cigarette. "You wants the panda, friend, youse is gotta earn the panda."

Andre shook his head and turned to Gwen as if to say, *Would you get a load of this guy?* Gwen smiled back and pointed her little finger at the big bear, making her desires absolutely clear. She wanted a panda.

Andre smiled, nodded, and turned back to the attendant. "Okay, what do I have to do to win the panda?"

The attendant cleaned his dirty fingernails with a toothpick. "Well, I'm glad you asked me that, friend. See, three balls is two dollars, but it takes ten balls to win the big ol' bear. Now, I tell youse what I am gonna do, friend," the attendant continued. Andre got the sense that the only thing the attendant was really going to do was try to fleece him for all the money he could. "Seeing as how youse gots yourself such a pretty lady over there, friend, I'll make youse a special deal. Seven more balls for the bargain basement price of five more dollars. What do ya say to that, friend?"

Andre did the math in his head. If three balls were two dollars then seven more balls should cost . . . "Some deal," he responded, reaching into his pocket for more money.

Gwen smiled again, enjoying the chivalry of Andre's valiant efforts to win her a giant panda. Andre rolled his eyes and laid the money down on the counter, and the attendant lined up seven more basketballs.

Andre picked up the first ball and got ready to

shoot. Suddenly the attendant put his hand up to stop him.

"Wait a minute, friend. One more thing. Youse is gots to step back and shoot from the blue line."

"What blue line?" Andre asked, turning his head. Sure enough there was a small strip of blue tape on the grass that looked as if it were a piece of trash discarded among the hot dog wrappers and soda cups strewn all over the ground.

"What?" Andre asked. "Why? I just shot from the red line."

"Yep, ya sure did, friend. But that was before I knew youse was a panda person. See, panda people shoot from the blue line and now youse is a panda person, you see?" The attendant lit his third cigarette off the end of his second, then tossed the butt onto the grass and stomped it out. Andre was sure the soccer players who used the field regularly would be thrilled to find that next week.

"Man, what kind of garbage are you trying to pull on me?" asked Andre.

"Ain't no garbage, friend. Dem's the rules. I don't make 'em, and you can't break 'em. But if youse wants to call it quits, you can just take one of those little beauties over there. How about a nice squirrel pencil sharpener for your sweetheart? You think a pretty gal like that would want a squirrel pencil sharpener?"

Andre paused and looked this con man over.

"Oh, come on, friend, you look like a ringer. Win your pretty a panda. Youse ain't gonna get her nothing if you don't try and then she might not give youse nothing for not tryin', if ya know what I mean." The attendant took another deep puff and looked Gwen over from top to bottom. Appearing to like what he saw, he continued on, speaking through the cigarette smoke as he exhaled. "Yep, real special. She's got to be something mighty unique to go out with a guy like you. Mighty unique," he said in a slow, suggestive drawl. "Now, go on, friend, win the lady a panda."

The attendant smirked, his snide remark obviously intended to annoy Andre and bait him into losing his composure. Andre stared at the attendant, looked back at Gwen and then back at the attendant one more time.

Andre put the ball down, peeled off his jacket and handed it to Gwen. There was a gleam in his eye.

"That's the way, friend," the attendant answered, happy to see another sucker about to be served up on the carnival's platter.

Andre picked the ball up and took two steps

back to the blue line. The blue-line shot wasn't nearly as easy as the red-line shot, and with the bent rim and the carnival's lopsided rubber basketballs, there was little margin for error.

Andre dribbled the ball a few times to get the feel and set his gaze on the rim with a steely focus. A small crowd gathered to watch.

He let the first shot fly. *SWISH!* The attendant passed him the next ball. *SWISH!* And then another and another and another. *SWISH! SWISH! SWISH!*

The attendant paused before passing Andre the next ball. He thought about saying something, because Andre was now at eight in a row, but he didn't, and simply passed Andre the next ball. The crowd was growing bigger.

SWISH!

"All right, hotshot, them's nine in a row," the attendant said, growing angry. "One more and youse gets the bear."

The attendant slowly passed Andre the ball. It was a bad pass, low and at Andre's knees, a pathetic attempt to disrupt Andre's rhythm.

"Sorry about that, friend."

Andre didn't waste any energy responding.

A hush went over the crowd. Twenty-five or so people were now watching, all silently rooting for

Andre. Andre lifted the ball to shoot. He raised his arms and—

"Don't choke, friend," the attendant interrupted. "Be a shame to see the pressure get to ya."

"*¡Ay, idiota!*" Gwen cursed under her breath in response to what the attendant was trying to do.

Andre pulled the ball back down. The attendant spit a nasty goober onto the grass and rubbed it in with his shoe. He was a disgusting man, and he didn't care who knew it.

Andre scanned the crowd. He looked at Gwen, the panda, the people gathered, and then the rim. He brought his gaze back to the basketball and dribbled once.

Andre looked up, locked in on the basket, and let it fly. . . . *SWISH!* Nothing but net.

A roar went through the crowd.

"Yeah!" Gwen exclaimed as she ran up and jumped into Andre's arms, smothering him with hugs and kisses, smiling all the while. A few people in the crowd clapped. Others walked away satisfied, as if they had just seen a great show. They mumbled things like "The man can sure shoot."

Gwen stuck out her arm and proudly pointed to her bear. "*Oye*, that one!" she said with extra zest. The attendant slumped his head and took out a stepladder.

With no energy whatsoever he took down the giant panda and handed it to Gwen.

"*Gracias*, friend," she said as she snatched it out of his arms.

Andre put on his jacket, smiled, and the two of them walked away. Gwen hugged her new bear as if it were the best present anybody had ever given her.

"That was great. I love amusement parks. Let's get out of here," Gwen said.

"Right now?" Andre asked. "But we'll miss the big fireworks show."

"I promise, you won't miss a thing," she offered with a sly look.

"Right. We're outta here," Andre said.

"Lead the way," Gwen said, squeezing her bear one more time. "Ah, my hero."

XI

Gwen held her panda bear tightly as she and Andre walked hand in hand over an old tire, past an abandoned flagpole, and beyond a craggy fence that looked as if it had been crumpled for some time.

"How do you know about this place?" Gwen inquired as she carefully sidestepped a hose.

"It's my old clubhouse," Andre responded, hopping over a cement block. The terrain really wasn't too bad though, and Andre seemed to be enjoying stepping over the broken pieces of PVC pipe and discarded soda bottles, as if making his way through this mini obstacle course was in some way a reliving of his old life. "Here's the door," he said after a final skip.

Andre stopped and gave Gwen a kiss. It was a long, deep kiss that was obviously heading somewhere well beyond the lips. Their lips parted and Andre turned toward the entrance.

"Hey," Gwen casually asked as Andre reached for the door. "That stuff the hillbilly guy was talkin' at the shooting gallery bother you?"

"No. He's an idiot. Bother you?"

"Mmm," she said, "didn't really think about it."

Andre paused.

"Actually, you did think about it," Andre said, taking his hand off the doorknob. "I mean, that's why you asked, isn't it?"

"Asked what?" Gwen inquired. "I mean, I wanna make sure we're talking about the same thing."

"Is this about the fact that we're . . . you know— I'm black, right?"

"What are you trying to say? I mean, I'm here, ain't I?"

"But you think about it, don't you?"

"Well, obviously you do too, otherwise we wouldn't be having this conversation right now. True? *¿Sí o no?*"

"Of course I think about. All of society thinks about it," Andre responded, ready to explore the issue further. But Gwen, sensing the mood shift, decided to change course.

"Look, do you want to talk *tontería* or do you want to talk"—Gwen slid closer to Andre and whispered softly into his ear—"*amor?*"

When Gwen's tongue sensually entered Andre's ear, his seriousness melted away faster than an ice cube in a microwave. He quickly remembered where he was and why he was there. He threw open the door to the clubhouse. To his surprise, to everyone's surprise, Andre found a light on and the whole room filled with smoke.

He peeked inside. Across the room Theresa, Andre's sister, sat on an old bar stool smoking an unevenly rolled joint. Two of her girlfriends, Lasheena and Sonji, relaxed on the couch across from her, stoned out of their minds. The pungent scent of marijuana explained everything.

"Whew! Am I glad it's just you," Theresa said, exhaling smoke. "I had no idea who it might be."

"Like the bogey man and shit," added Lasheena. All three girls giggled.

"What the hell are you doing here?" Andre asked.

Theresa pulled a lighter from her pocket. "We's just having a kick-back. You know, takin' a break before the big fireworks show," she said as she relit the joint she had been smoking prior to being interrupted.

"Yeah, just chillin' before the show," added Sonji.

"Chillin' like villains. Gimme some," Lasheena said as she reached for the joint.

"Cool out a second, girl," Theresa replied.

"I mean," Andre said evenly, "what the hell are you doing?"

"Just takin' a couple of tokes. Want some?" Theresa asked, offering Andre the pot.

"No, I don't want some!" Andre snapped.

"All right, all right. Chill out," Theresa responded slowly.

"Don't tell me to chill out," Andre snapped once more.

"Okay! Okay! Jesus Christ, Andre. It ain't no big thang," Theresa said casually.

"It ain't a big thang, but I still want to smoke it, so pass that bad-boy blunt over here, girlfriend," Sonji demanded as she reached for the joint.

"Ain't no big thing? Ain't no big thing? Theresa, what the hell is going on in your brain?" Andre shouted.

"Sensimilla, mon," Lasheena added in a Jamaican accent. The three girls giggled some more. Andre wasn't laughing.

"Aw, mellow out, Andre. It ain't like you ain't never smoked pot before," Theresa said in a superior sort of voice.

"Sure, when I was young and stupid," Andre countered.

"Yeah, I know, I know. First it's dope, then the next thing I know I'm hitting the crack pipe or shooting heroin and turnin' into some bag lady who eats lunch out of a Dumpster or something."

"I didn't say that," Andre replied.

Theresa rose to her feet, hunched over, and limped toward the garbage can. She began to sift through the rubbish, impersonating a bag lady looking for scraps.

In a cracked voice she shook her finger at everyone in the room. "Maybe there's an old chicken bone or some welfare cheese in here. Oh, if only I would have stayed away from mary-juana. If only I never smoked that July Fourth joint. Woe is me!"

Lasheena and Sonji nearly fell off the couch laughing.

"That's real funny. Real funny, Theresa," Andre said.

Theresa quickly straightened up and shot back with a healthy dose of attitude in her voice, "That's right! It is real funny. Looky, you ain't my father, so don't be trying to tell me what to do, ya hear?"

"You'd better watch who you're snappin' at," Andre barked.

"All I'm doing is kickin' it back on a holiday weekend, so get out of my face with that don't-do-drugs speech. It's tired, Andre. Real tired. Just like you."

"Come here! Come here, little girl. I'll show you who—"

Andre lunged toward Theresa, but Gwen stepped in front of him and held him back.

"Let's go, Andre. *Vamos*. Let's get out of here and forget it," Gwen said, trying to calm the situation down.

"No! I'm not forgetting nothing," Andre thundered. "That's the problem. Everyone just wants to forget about it."

"Let's just go," Gwen insisted as she tried to pull Andre toward the door. He was too strong for her, though, and didn't want to go.

"No, I ain't going anywhere," Andre snapped. "Drugs are bringing down our whole damned country. Especially black people. We're self-destructing from the whole 'Let's just forget about it' mentality, so do not start on me with that pathetically sad song about how I should just forget about this. I'm forgetting nothing. It's a thing that we have got to start dealing with."

"Oh, I see. And I suppose a little ol' Chicana girl like me couldn't even begin to understand a big ol' black problem like this," Gwen said.

"That's not what I said," Andre responded.

"*Mierda del toro* and the hell it wasn't!" Gwen fired back.

"Sure sounded like dat to me," Sonji piped in from her side of the couch.

134

"Uh-huh, sho' did," replied Lasheena as she gave a high five to Sonji. "*Mee-er-doo de la tor-doo* and hasta la pasta, too!" The girls laughed.

"Oh, I know you are not steppin' to me with mockery, little girl!" Gwen barked in a voice full of Latina pride as she turned toward the two girls on the couch.

"Naw, naw, we cool, *señorita*. Chill, we cool. Brown and black is bonded. We tight. I mean, you could kick me some Ebonics smack if ya want," Sonji offered.

"Yeah, like"—Lasheena sat up straight and puffed out her chest—"we be wantin' to be free be of the prejudice be."

Sonji and Theresa nearly bust their ribs laughing at Lasheena's Ebonics imitation. Gwen just shook her head.

"I wouldn't stoop so low."

Andre glared at the girls and then turned to Gwen. He could see she was flaming mad. "Oh, come on, Gwen. You know it's not like that."

"Go screw your teddy bear!" she snapped as she hurled the giant panda at Andre. The bear bounced off Andre's head and landed sideways on the floor in a puddle of mud.

Gwen stormed out of the clubhouse and

slammed the door behind her. Andre started after her.

"Gwen!" he called out. "Wait a minute. That's not what I meant!" But she didn't turn around.

Andre stopped at the front door to look back at the girls. Theresa reached for the lighter on the counter.

"Damn, if that ain't humiliating," she remarked as she looked at the panda bear lying on the floor, its white coat already filthy.

Theresa relit the joint and passed it to Lasheena. Andre looked at the bear, looked at his sister, looked at her friends, and shook his head. Then he left.

"Ooh, girl, you told him," Sonji said as she reached for another toke.

"Think he messin' with some little girl," she remarked. *"Shee-it!"*

The sound of the door slamming behind Andre made all three of them giggle once again.

"Hasta la pasta. Dat's a funny one, girl."

XII

Empty juice glasses, plates with random crumbs, and a half bowl of four-night-old cereal sat strewn across Andre's desk. While he was usually somewhat neat, cleanliness wasn't really a major issue for him at this point. His only concern was that he had been at his desk hunched over his writing space for so many hours in a row, it felt as if he were starting to grow a hump.

Andre lifted his pen from the paper, stopped, and read over what he had written. Dissatisfied, he ripped the sheet from his notebook and crumpled it into a tight ball. He swiveled in his chair and turned toward the little garbage can, intent on sinking a basket. He turned, focused on the basket, set to shoot, and . . . missed. The ball of paper dinked off the rim of the wastebasket and found a home next to the other shots he'd sprinkled across the floor that hadn't gone in either.

Andre turned back around and faced his notebook. He flipped a few sheets back and read over some other pages he had written. With a shake of his head he turned off the light, backed away from his desk, and crawled into bed. Crafting words to express the combination of rage, frustration, and disappointment he felt, commingled with the ideas of hope, optimism, and possibility he wanted to infuse into his writing was proving to be a grueling task. Once again, it was after three in the morning.

Andre pulled back the covers and collapsed, exhausted. But just as soon as his head hit the pillow he climbed right back out of bed and turned on the desk light yet again. He opened his notebook, picked up his pen, and stuck the back end in his mouth, where he could chew on the pen cap. Andre was always a better writer when he was chewing on the pen cap. It was less than a week before Mr. Jarvin's deadline, but time wasn't his real concern—inspiration was.

And suddenly, Andre found it.

He began to write. Once he had started, he didn't stop for about seventy-five minutes. Oblivious to the time, he finished his final sentence, reached around his desk and turned on his computer. As soon as the machine was ready, Andre began to type.

I am a racist. I am a bigot. I am a man who judges people by the color of their skin. If a black person approaches me as I walk down the street at night, they are to be feared. If a Hispanic person does not speak English while shopping in a store, they are an illegal. If a white person pays for a cup of coffee with a twenty-dollar bill, they are wealthy. As I said, I am a racist. I am a bigot.

And I am wrong.

I am so, so wrong.

XIII

Andre sat in the chair with his hands folded in his lap while he waited. And waited. Andre was learning that having another person read what you have written is tough enough, but to have them read it while you are in the room watching them read it is excruciating. Every twitch of the nose, every piece of dust in Mr. Jarvin's eye became more than just a twitch of the nose or a piece of dust. It became for Andre a full-blown dialogue in his head about how much Mr. Jarvin hated his work. Heaven forbid the big boss got the desire to tug on his earlobe or rub his chin, because Andre would have misinterpreted this as a nonverbal signal for him to change occupational aspirations immediately and become a plumber. Andre hated plumbing. After ten minutes of torture the only real question Andre had left in his head was how loud a *bzzzt* he was going to get.

Mr. Jarvin finished the last words on the page and slowly peered over his glasses at Andre. He opened his mouth to speak but stopped himself. He pushed his glasses back up his nose and then perused the piece again. Andre waited.

After scanning the article one more time Mr. Jarvin removed his glasses from his face and turned to Andre.

"Are you proud of this?" he asked.

"Well, I—"

"Well, you should be, Andre. You should be damned proud of this," Mr. Jarvin continued without waiting for Andre to finish his sentence. "To tell you the truth, this is more than I was looking for. It's simple. It's smart. It's got understanding and feeling and guts. But most important, it's from the heart."

"Thank you, Mr. Jarvin. I am glad you like it," Andre replied, trying to remain polite. Though he wanted to feel proud, on the inside Andre was still waiting for a *bzzzt*.

"Like it?" Mr. Jarvin bellowed. "Andre, are you listening to what I am saying? I'm a professional magazine editor. I don't blow smoke up people's asses, they blow it up mine. I am telling you, this is excellent. Originally, I figured at best we'd have to spend a few weeks polishing it up and trimming it down, you know, slashing this and laying waste to that to get it right. But it is right. It's damned right."

Mr. Jarvin crossed his room and looked out his window.

"Okay, what to do, what to do?" he said, more to himself than Andre. "First," Mr. Jarvin said, shooting back around, "go over to Suzie in the photo department and have her take a couple of pictures for an insert. Hell, with a slight polish, this can make it in the next issue. Yeah, and with the title on the front cover and your name right beside it. Everyone who reads our magazine is going to know that this piece was written by our hot new writer, Andre Anderson. That's what we'll do. What do you think of that, Andre?"

"Well, I think that's—"

"Of course you do. And I tell you something else," Mr. Jarvin added, talking a mile a minute. "I think this is going to be a big success. A big success."

Mr. Jarvin turned and paused, again lost in his thoughts as he pieced his vision of the puzzle together.

"Do you think I should—"

"The only thing I think you should do," barked Mr. Jarvin, "is go and see Suzie right now and tell her to take some pictures of you. I don't care where she takes them, but tell her I want them shot in black and white. Black and white, you hear?"

"Yeah, I got it," Andre responded, still sitting in his chair.

"Well, what are you waiting for, a banana peel? Slide on over to Suzie's desk and take those pictures," Mr. Jarvin ordered as he zipped to his chair and picked up the telephone. "We still have a million things to do, Andre. When you've got something hot, you got to go with it *tout de suite*. That's French for 'right away.' So go, go, go!"

Andre rose from his chair and left. He didn't walk out of the office, though. . . . He floated.

The picture on the magazine cover was the seal of the President of the United States. In bold letters the title read, "The Seven Most Important Things the President Does in a Week."

Across the bottom of the cover in stylized print were the words: "Also Inside: *Where Are All the Detectives?* by J. Evan Lomar; *The Working Weekenders* by Sharon Coles; *My Brothers* by Andre Anderson."

Smoke rose from behind the leather chair. Slowly swiveling around was Mr. Jarvin, sucking on a huge cigar. In his hands he held a stack of letters.

"So, what's it feel like to be a raging success?" Mr. Jarvin asked, taking another puff of his cigar. "I've got more mail on you than this place has seen in months."

Mr. Jarvin pulled a random letter from the pile and read it aloud. "'One of the most compassionate and articulate articles your magazine has ever published. Congratulations to Mr. Anderson.'"

Mr. Jarvin grabbed another letter. "'Refreshing, positive, and straightforward. Qualities long forgotten in the debates about race and prejudice.'"

Another read, "'Bravo, Andre. Bravo!'" Mr. Jarvin's bravura reading caused Andre to blush a little, but Jarvin kept going.

"Oh here, I love this one," the boss said as he fumbled through the stack until he came across the letter he was looking for. "'When it comes to race relations I consider myself disillusioned, sad, angry, and confused. So tell me, Andre, why do I feel so refreshed? P.S. Renew my subscription for a lifetime.'" Mr. Jarvin beamed with pride. "Andre, are you listening to this? I'm promoting you. A bigger contributing credit, a parking pass, a raise, a new desk . . ." He paused.

Andre jumped in. "Well, I don't know about the new desk part. I mean, space is so limited already."

"Always the team player, huh? Don't sweat it,

I'm sure we'll find something." The telephone rang. "One second, Andre. Yeah, this is Jarvin."

A dark, ominous voice came through the receiver.

"Printing that nigger-loving shit is only going to cause problems for you and your magazine. Don't do it anymore."

"What? Hello? Who is this?" Jarvin demanded.

"All mistakes need to be rectified. Don't make any more." *Click.* The line went dead.

Mr. Jarvin pulled the phone away from his ear and stared vacantly into space for a minute, not quite sure what to think.

"Something wrong, Mr. Jarvin?" Andre asked.

The sound of Andre's voice brought Mr. Jarvin back from the abyss of his thoughts. He shook his head and did his best to pretend that everything was all right.

"What? Oh, um, no. Yeah, everything's good. Just a few fans of yours, I guess."

"Excuse me?" Andre asked.

"Aw, nothing. Where was I?" Mr. Jarvin mumbled absentmindedly, trying to get back to where he had been moments before.

"My promotion," Andre answered, not forgetting at all. This was a dream come true for Andre. Though the idea of more money and a parking pass was nice, the bigger credit on the magazine's mast-head was what really had his heart jumping.

"Ah, right. No more photocopying and filing for you, it's on to the bigger and better. You're on assignment now. Strictly human-interest stuff. We'll get you a computer, a good chair—every writer needs a good chair—plus, I think you'll find the raise in pay agree-able," Mr. Jarvin said with a wink. "What do you say, Andre?"

Andre opened his mouth to speak.

"Good, I knew you'd say that," Mr. Jarvin said. "Now, you can start by thinking of a follow-up article. Find a good slant. Here, take some of this mail," Mr. Jarvin said as he passed Andre an untidy pile of let-ters. "Look through it and see what you think. Maybe an idea will jump out at you."

Mr. Jarvin tossed a few more letters that had been lying on his desk into Andre's outstretched arms.

"I don't know what to say about all of this," Andre remarked. "It all feels like it is happening so quickly."

"That's because it is," Mr. Jarvin responded. "Wait, I have an idea. Why don't you call your next piece 'My Sisters'? Yeah, that's it. And we'll do another one after that called 'My Fathers.' And then

'My Mothers.' Hey, how about a piece called 'My Cousins Three Times Removed'? I think we're on to something here."

With a grin on his face Andre turned to leave. "Think about it, Andre, we can milk this one all the way to 'My Great-Great-Step-Niece's Aunt.'"

"I'll work on it, Mr. Jarvin," Andre said as he shook his head and closed the office door. Andre felt good. He knew that at *Affairs* magazine, there was something to be said for being respected enough by Mr. Jarvin to have him tease you.

Andre crossed to his desk, his old desk, where he thought he heard the phone ringing, but when he got there he realized that it was the phone at the desk next to his. Andre tossed down the stack of mail given to him by Mr. Jarvin and started to flip through the letters. The phone on the next desk kept ringing. He tried to concentrate on the mail, but his sense of duty got the better of him and he tossed down the letters that were in his hand and crossed over to answer the ringing phone. It was somebody looking for somebody else across the hall and, of course, Andre was asked to relay a message about something and somebody to someone about something, which he happily did.

Andre tossed the remainder of the stack of

unread mail on his desk and exited. As he went off dutifully to relay the phone message, he failed to see that one of the letters he had been holding had been sent to him from the PPA.

XIV

It was nighttime when Andre pulled into the driveway of his house. His home was completely dark. This puzzled him. Something didn't feel right.

He climbed out of his car and looked around. An eerie silence filled the air. Andre felt a shiver run through him, but shook it off. He pulled out his key and walked boldly toward his front door.

A rustle in the bushes made him jump. He peered into the darkness but couldn't see anything. He stood as still as a thief and listened intently, but after a moment or two, when he heard no further sound, Andre turned back around and stepped toward the door.

Suddenly, someone grabbed him from behind.

"Hey! What the—"

A face appeared out of the darkness. It was Cedric. "Yo, it's me, Andre. Calm down, dude."

It took a second for Andre to realize who it was. "Holy Jesus, Cedric, you scared the hell out of me!" Andre snapped.

"Sorry, man," Cedric responded in a soft voice. "I just wanted to, you know, chat with you a minute, about that thing that happened. You know, that thing the last time. I just, you know, wanted to . . . apologize."

Cedric paused and looked down. Andre took a deep breath, exhaled slowly, and shook off his fright.

"Aw, it's cool, Ced," he responded. "It was kind of my fault, too. That whole situation just got way out of hand."

Cedric raised his eyes to look at Andre. Neither of them knew what else to say or do, and there was an awkward pause. Cedric kicked a pebble off the porch.

"I just hope I didn't bust you up too bad," Andre added.

Cedric looked up and saw that Andre was grinning. Andre faked a quick left hook and Cedric flinched. Then a big smile came over both their faces.

"Mess me up? Damn, I was worried I did some permanent damage to your already damaged face," Cedric countered as he playfully poked Andre in the chest.

"What? This face? Man, get outta here. This is a great face," Andre said, propping up his chin.

Both of them laughed at the way Andre

stuck out his chin, and then exchanged one of their patented up-around-and-over high fives.

"You know," Cedric continued, "I read what you wrote for that magazine. That stuff was great, man. Freakin' great."

"You can read, Ced?" Andre joked.

"No, for real. I ain't jesting with ya, Andre," Cedric continued, trying to keep it serious for a minute. "What you said, you know, about everybody having to ask what's important to them and figure out a way to, you know, uphold their own responsibility. That stuff was like . . . you know, it was like gospel, but without the preacher. I mean, I never read nothing worded like that before."

"Thanks, Ced," Andre replied.

"Naw, you got skills, cuz. You're gifted," Cedric continued. "That's why I felt extra bad about what went down between us. I mean I thought about it and all and maybe, you know, you're sorta right. I'm-a cut some of that garbage out of my act."

"Even the watermelon joke?" Andre asked in a serious tone.

Cedric paused. "Well . . ." Cedric fumbled over his response. "I'll change some of the material but, it's like, you know—"

"'Cause you shouldn't cut that one. That one

was funny," Andre replied with a sly look. Andre reached over to put Cedric in a playful headlock, but Cedric was too quick and escaped.

"Yo, wait a sec, *all* of it is funny. Just some might be a bit, how do I say it, *too* funny. Yeah, that's it. It's too funny," Cedric repeated, liking the ring of it.

"You keep telling yourself that," Andre replied as he reached for his key and unlocked the door. "I wonder where everyone is?" he said as he twisted open the doorknob and turned on the light.

"Surprise!" Seventy-five people popped out from behind curtains, couches and lampshades, catching Andre completely off guard. Aunt Marie snapped a picture, blinding Andre with the flash, while his mother rushed forward and smothered him with kisses and presented a homemade cake. The inscription read CONGRATULATIONS, ANDRE and there was a little pen and piece of parchment paper drawn in red icing.

Aunt Marie snapped another few pictures. Andre was soon completely blinded by the flashing light.

"Woman, gimme that camera," Pops said to his sister Marie. "You just took three pictures of my ceiling."

"Hush up, I did not."

All sorts of people from Andre's life swarmed

up to him and wished him their best. The whole family, Shawn, Andre's basketball buddies, people from the magazine office, everyone had come to celebrate Andre's good fortune.

A new employee at the magazine whose name Andre couldn't recall (it was either Riley or Raymond) came up to him holding a big plate of homemade ribs and corn. "Hey, congrats, Andre. Wow, someone around here sure can cook."

"Thanks. Yeah, that would be my mom," Andre responded as Riley/Raymond wandered off to get a drink.

Andre looked around, apparently seeking someone in particular, when Josephine, the plump neighbor who always knew everybody's business whether or not she knew what she was talking about, walked up to Andre and gave him a smooch on his cheek, leaving a wedge of gaudy red lipstick on his face in her wake. "I always knew you was gonna do some good."

"Thanks, Jojo. Thanks a lot," Andre replied, still scanning the crowd.

More people smothered Andre with kisses and hugs and congratulations until the rumor mill had it that Mrs. Anderson was cutting her cake in the kitchen. Since it was Mrs. Anderson's homemade triple-chocolate layer cake being served, the crowd around Andre dispersed instantly and people headed off to the kitchen to make sure they got a piece. It was nice that Andre was a writer, but when it came to Mrs. Anderson's cake, Charles Dickens would have been abandoned just as quickly.

"'Scuse me, Brother," said Lorenzo as he good-naturedly pushed his way past a tie-wearing white guy from *Affairs* whom he didn't know. "Reading is good, but eatin' is better."

Andre was still peering through the crowd when Shawn approached with a huge mound of cake on his plate.

"Good job, buddy!" he said as he shoveled a forkful of food into his mouth.

"Thanks," Andre said as he looked around the room a bit more. "Say, you didn't happen to speak with . . ."

"Gwen? Yeah. She never wants you to call her again," Shawn answered as he plowed some more cake into his mouth. Andre looked at him closely, and for a moment the whole party melted away and his heart sunk. Was Shawn serious?

"Nawww . . ." he said, enjoying the fact that he could so easily mess with Andre's mind. "She wanted to come, but she felt really bad about some fight you two had and wanted to speak to you alone. She told me to give you a big kiss and to have you call her tomorrow."

Shawn quickly wrapped his arm around Andre and gave him a huge, juicy, wet, cake-filled kiss on the cheek before Andre could squirm away.

"Man, get away from me," Andre protested. Dabbles of chocolate hung from Andre's face.

"That's from her. She made me promise," Shawn said as Andre wiped the goo off his cheek.

Cedric walked past with two plates of cake but only one fork. Andre didn't have to be a detective to figure out what was going on there.

"Is that good?" Andre asked, referring to Shawn's cake.

"Mmm-hmmm," Shawn responded and then rammed another bite into his mouth. He stretched his face so wide it looked as if his lips were going to tear at the seams.

"Gimme a bite," Andre said, reaching for Shawn's plate.

Shawn got defensive. "Nnuh-unnhhh," he said as he turned his back to Andre and scampered off into the center of the party. "Hey, Mrs. A., cut me off a corner piece. Everybody knows I taught him how to write."

155

Andre took another look around and noticed all the smiles filling the room.

"Woman, would you give me that camera?" The flash went off. "Now, look what you did," exclaimed Pops. "You just took a picture of my lamp."

Andre couldn't help but smile. People were partying, eating, laughing, and having an old-fashioned good time. One look around showed him in no uncertain terms what he had always known—he was a loved young man.

XV

It was a new day at the office. Andre hustled around his spankingly magnificent desk completely energized. Well, maybe the desk wasn't really "spankingly magnificent," but to Andre it was a mahogany masterpiece any CEO would be proud to sit behind. He shuffled through papers, wrote quick notes to himself, and opened and closed his new drawers like a pro. If someone had walked by, they might have mistaken him for a VIP in a major corporation.

A telephone rang in the background. Rene, the proofreader, answered it.

"Hey, Andre. Line three, for you," she called out.

"Thanks, Rene, I have it," he said as he picked up the phone. "This is Andre."

"Ooh, so official."

Andre melted when he heard her voice.

"I was hoping you would call."

"Hi," said Gwen.

"Hi," replied Andre.

Gwen stood in a phone booth with one hand covering her free ear to shield it from all the noise. Kids from camp ran around screaming at the tops of their lungs behind her.

"I've been trying to get in touch with you," Andre said softly as he took a seat.

"What?" Gwen shouted. A little girl pressed her face against the door of the phone booth and smushed her nose so tight against the glass that she left a trail of snot when she finally walked away. "It's really hard to hear you."

Andre put down the pen in his hand and tried to find a place to begin. "I said, how are you?"

"I'm good. *¿Y tú?*"

"I'm good."

"Sorry I'm calling from here, but I haven't had much time lately," Gwen continued. "Do you want to meet me at the Shoebox Café around eight o'clock tonight?"

"Sure, sure, at the Shoebox Cafe. Eight is perfect," Andre said. "That will give me some extra time around the office. I was planning on staying a bit late tonight anyway."

There was a pause.

"Hey, Gwen, I—I hope you know . . ."

A cute little camper whose shoes were untied

started banging on the phone booth glass. "I gotta go pee-pee," she said.

"Andre, we'll have to talk later," Gwen cut in. "I'm sorry. I want to talk, I just have to get back right now."

"Um, yeah. Okay," Andre replied.

"I'll see you at eight," Gwen said as the little camper kept banging and banging. "G'bye."

"Yep, see you then," Andre answered.

Although he hung up the phone, there were about a thousand things more he had wanted to say. Andre stared blankly off in the distance thinking about all of them. There was apologizing, clearing the air, explaining his feelings for her, vowing to make things better, his desire to kiss her again and again, and on and on and on. A gajillion thoughts were scrambled in his brain all at the same time, but after about a minute or so, another phone rang at a desk across the way and woke him from his daze. Andre scooped up the papers he was looking at, flipped open his spiral notebook, popped the pen cap back into his mouth, and went back to work. After all, he had work to do.

Reading from the top of a tall stack of papers, Andre exited the building into the office's parking area. The garage was empty except for a few scattered vehicles here and there and the sound of Andre's footsteps across the empty parking lot made a sort of lyrical *click, click* echoing throughout the underground structure. If he hurried, he wouldn't be late to meet Gwen at the café. He walked to his car at a brisk pace.

"Is that him?" Inside a beat-up old van five men watched Andre cross the garage.

The man in the driver's seat lifted a copy of *Affairs* magazine and matched the picture to the person.

"Yeah, it looks like the guy in the photo."

The others waited for the man in the front passenger seat to give the word. The man in the front looked at his watch—it was an expensive watch made in a foreign country—and he polished the face of the crystal by rubbing it softly across his sleeve.

"All right, let's do this," he said. The driver turned on the van.

After fumbling for his keys, Andre approached his car and opened the driver's door. Suddenly, the van screeched up alongside him.

Startled, Andre looked up, and before he knew what was happening, four burly white men were jumping out of the sliding panel door. Andre quickly looked around and realized there was nobody else in the garage.

"Is there some kind of problem?" Andre asked, understanding there obviously was.

"Yeah, the bullshit you write," one of them said. "But that is about to stop."

The first guy stepped up and threw a punch at Andre's face, but Andre was too quick. He dropped his papers, ducked, and instinctively retaliated with an overhand left that cracked the man in the center of his face. *Pop!*

"Oow! My freakin' nose!"

"Look, I don't want any trouble," Andre said as he became more closely surrounded. Though Andre didn't know who these guys were—he knew who these guys were.

"Neither do we," said another of the men, then one of the others threw a sloppy punch that nailed Andre in the stomach. Andre buckled over, but before he could recover his breath, three guys pounced on top of him, overwhelming him with body blows and shots to the head.

The first guy, the one Andre had pummeled, walked up to the car mirror and inspected his mangled features. "Look at my face! Hold that black bastard!"

Andre struggled, but he was overpowered. The four men started working Andre over with extra vigor, when suddenly the passenger-side van door opened and a calm voice said in a soft tone, "That's enough."

Though their energy was high and their adrenaline was flowing, all four men immediately stopped. The only thing that could be heard in the circle around Andre was the heavy breathing of his attackers.

The leader walked up and raised Andre's face by lifting him at the scruff of his shirt to inspect the damage. Andre was in bad shape.

"You know, Mr. Anderson, you have a very nice style about your work," the leader began. "It's, dare I say, sophisticated."

The leader nodded his head as some sort of sign. The four brutes immediately understood whatever the signal meant and they sprang into action. Methodically, they carried Andre over to his car and hoisted him up near his open driver's-side door. With a thin rope, the men quickly laced up Andre's wrist and fingers. Pulling the rope tight they stretched Andre's right arm out in such a way that his hand was restrained yet fully extended over the doorjamb.

"But everybody knows, Mr. Anderson," the

leader continued, "that truly great writing is not about style. It is about substance. Consider this a little literary tip. Don't write any more of that nigger shit!"

Bam! The leader slammed the car door on Andre's hand, violently crushing his bones in the doorjamb. Andre screamed in pain.

The leader opened the car door again. Andre struggled to pull away, but he couldn't, because his wrist was tied. *BAM!*

BAM! BAM!

BAM!

Everything stopped. Satisfied, the leader nodded his head and the other men cut Andre loose. Andre collapsed to the ground, dragged his mangled right hand toward the pit of his belly, and cradled it like a baby. He lay crumpled up on the asphalt in the fetal position, shaking, and rocking softly back and forth. The men hurried back into the van. The leader stayed back for a moment, glanced around the empty parking lot, kneeled and grabbed the semiconscious Andre by the roots of his hair. He lifted Andre's face off the ground and then whispered into his ear.

"Next time, it will be your head."

The leader let go of Andre's hair and his head fell to the ground with a disquieting thump. The leader straightened up, smoothed out his slacks, and calmly walked around to the passenger-side door of the vehicle and climbed in.

The van sped away. Andre was left lying on the cold pavement hunched over in a pool of blood and papers.

XVI

The hospital hallway was sterile and cold. Nurses and doctors swiftly moved around in purposeful silence.

Mrs. Anderson and Pops rushed up to the reception area, frantically questioning the lady behind the desk.

"Where's my baby? Is he all right? What room is he in?" Mrs. Anderson pleaded.

The nurse, emotionless, looked up from behind a stack of files. This must have been her thirty-second emergency of the day.

"What is his name, ma'am?" she asked.

"His name is Andre," Pops answered. "Andre Anderson."

The nurse flipped through a chart hanging from a clip on the wall. When she found what she was looking for, she looked back at the Anderson family and paused. It was as if she were deciding something.

"One moment please," she said and then left her desk and began a long walk down a long hall.

Mrs. Anderson trembled so badly she could hardly stand. Pops grabbed her arm to make sure she didn't fall.

A moment later a young physician came walking out of a door at the other end of the corridor and began a brief conversation with the nurse. Although Pops couldn't hear what they actually said, he could tell by the way that the nurse had motioned with her head toward the Andersons that she was saying something that meant *That's them.*

The doctor nodded and began walking toward them.

"Mr. and Mrs. Anderson? My name is Dr. Solomon. I treated your son when he was brought here a few hours ago."

"Is Andre okay, doctor? Please tell me that he's okay," Mrs. Anderson beseeched through a face streaming with tears.

"Your son was beaten up pretty badly, Mrs. Anderson," Dr. Solomon began. "Apparently, he was attacked in a parking lot. A custodian found him and called for an ambulance, and when he got here, well—we've done the best that we could for him."

The tears were running at full flow down Mrs. Anderson's face. Pops was expressionless. Intently listening, but expressionless.

"Who did it, doctor?" Pops asked.

"Why? Why?" Mrs. Anderson wailed.

"I am sorry to say that, for right now, nobody knows. The police are working on it and I am sure that they will wish to speak to the two of you a bit later." Dr. Solomon was still a young enough man of medicine not to be immune to the pain that families feel when one of their loved ones has been hurt.

"Mr. Anderson. Mrs. Anderson. Whoever did this to your son was vicious. Brutally so. Andre has two broken ribs, a bruised kidney, a concussion, and possibly a fractured eye socket. But the most atrocious part—" The doctor paused and collected himself, trying to figure out a soft way to relate a hard fact. "The most atrocious part is that these, I don't know what to call them, these monsters, they seemed intent on mangling one of Andre's hands almost beyond recognition. The human hand, Mr. Anderson, has twenty-seven bones in it. They crushed twenty-three of them."

"They, they did what?" Mrs. Anderson stammered as if she were in some sort of terrible dream. "But why?"

"I am very sorry. Your son is asleep right now and will probably be sedated until well into tomorrow morning. I'll check back on him again then."

Although there was nothing more he could now do, the doctor nonetheless felt guilty that he had other patients to attend to. He knew that in the language of doctor–patient's family relationships, the words *nothing more to be done* did not translate to *feeling comforted by seeing the doctor exit the room.*

"Again, I am really very sorry. If you need anything . . ." Dr. Solomon's voice trailed off.

"Can we see him?" Pops asked.

"Well, he's sleeping right now."

"Oh, please, doctor. I have got to go see my baby," Mrs. Anderson pleaded.

Dr. Solomon, seeing the pain in their eyes, succumbed.

"Okay, but not too long. He is in room 308. It's down the hall to the right." The doctor even went a step further than he had planned and began the long, sad walk down the corridor with the Andersons.

Room 310. Room 309. Room 308. They arrived at the door. The doctor opened it slowly. Mrs. Anderson and Pops entered the room where everything, from the curtains to the sheets to the plastic armrests on the chair, was white.

Andre lay unconscious. His face was swollen. There was a lump underneath his right eye and a butterfly bandage over stitches on his forehead. While

Andre's left arm was free to dangle over the bed, his right arm was suspended by a pulley system, wrapped from the tip of the finger down to the edge of his elbow in what seemed like yards and yards of bandages.

It appeared that if Andre was breathing. It also appeared as if he was barely alive. Mrs. Anderson nearly fainted when she saw him.

Three days later Andre sat up in the hospital bed while Dr. Solomon checked the dilation of his pupils and the degree to which his facial wounds were healing.

Pops and Mrs. Anderson sat in the two chairs along each side of the bed while Shawn and Cedric paced the room like pipe bombs ready to explode. Gwen fidgeted in the corner. Mr. Jarvin, an overcoat thrown over his arm, couldn't sit still for a moment, either.

"Andre," Dr. Solomon began, "you suffered a pretty severe concussion, but no bones in your face were broken and, thankfully, your eyesight wasn't damaged either. Your head is still probably going to pound for a few more days, but there should be no long-term aftereffects."

The doctor looked to Andre for some sort of

acknowledgment, but Andre was stoic, staring straight ahead, unresponsive.

"I am sorry to say, though," Dr. Solomon continued, "that your hand—well, it's not in very good shape."

"How bad is it, doctor?" Mrs. Anderson asked.

"Our specialist is out of town on vacation right now, but when he gets back I am going to have Andre see him," the doctor responded, attempting to avoid the question.

"But it will get better, though. Right, doctor?" Mrs. Anderson continued. Like any mother, she was looking for all hope despite logical signs to the contrary. "I mean, he'll be able to use it again, right?" she pressed.

"The bones have been set properly, but I think our specialist will—"

"Oh, please, Dr. Solomon. Tell us the truth," she continued. Once again, the doctor's youth worked in favor of the Andersons. A more experienced physician might have been too jaded to explain the destruction of Andre's hand any further and simply would have passed the buck to the specialist. After all, many doctors, after years in the profession, view human bodies much the way mechanics view automobiles. When wrecks come into the shop, mechanics think about the parts and not about how the owner feels about the car.

Dr. Solomon, though, still had heart.

"I am an optimist, Mrs. Anderson, so I am going to say, yes, with extensive rehabilitation, Andre should be able to use his hand again to do small things, like grip a spoon or pick up a glass. That sort of thing."

"He'll be able to play ball again, won't he, doc? You know, shoot some hoops, right?" Cedric asked.

Dr. Solomon paused.

"No, I doubt it."

Upon hearing this, Andre continued to stare blankly into space without so much as batting an eyelash. Dr. Solomon waited for some sort of response from Andre, some expression, reaction, outburst, explosion, or reply. Anything, verbal or otherwise. He didn't get one. There was nothing.

The silence grew awkward and uncomfortable.

"The police, they mentioned they might stop by this afternoon," Dr. Solomon said to Andre, introducing a new topic of conversation to break the silence. "That is, of course, if you wish to speak to them."

Again, no response. Not a word. Not a motion. Nothing aside from an occasional blink.

"Well, I guess I'll leave you alone with your family and, well, if you need anything, I, um, I'll stop back by in a few hours." Dr. Solomon closed his medical chart. With still no response from Andre, he exited the room.

Nobody talked, but the silence spoke volumes. The air was tense, the mood somber. Finally, Cedric slammed his fist against the wall.

"Man, we gotta do something!"

"Yeah, like find out who did this," Shawn added.

"The police will find them," Gwen countered.

"The police? The police ain't gonna find jack!" Cedric roared. "What world are you living in, girl?"

"Yeah, this ain't just another stolen bicycle," Shawn blurted out. "We're talkin' about Andre almost being killed."

Cedric bobbed his head up and down, the fire burning deep within him. "Damned right! We can't let nobody get away with this. Nobody! I'm gonna find out who did this," Cedric said with absolute determination. "Gonna find 'em."

"And do what? Whatch'ya going to do then?" Gwen shot back, hot under the collar herself.

"I tell you what I am going to do," Cedric replied. "I am going to do what I have to do, that's what. I know some people. I'm-a get a few answers."

"Sounds to me like you are going to start a riot," Gwen responded as she crossed her arms.

"If that is what it takes, *mamacita*, I will go start a riot. I'll start a thousand riots!" Cedric ranted. "Stuff like this can't go on. Nuh-uh!"

"I am right there with you, Ced," Shawn said as he slapped hands with Cedric, like blood brothers taking an oath.

"Shut up! Just shut up, the two of you!" Pops yelled, jumping out of his chair. "You boys sound like ignorant fools, even to a deaf old man like me. There ain't gonna be no riots."

"What?" Cedric retorted. "I don't think I am hearing you right, Pops. That's your son lying there."

"Don't you tell me who is lying in that damned bed, boy," Pops snapped back angrily. He made a motion of walking toward Cedric, but Mrs. Anderson held him back. Actually, she *tried* to hold him back, but Pops pushed her arm away as if it weren't there, and continued moving forward.

"I love my son more than I love life itself, so don't remind me who is lying in that damn hospital bed right there. But if you would use your hard-to-find brain for a minute," Pops continued, "maybe you would understand what I am talking about. Didn't you read what he wrote? Didn't it mean something to you?"

Cedric straightened up. "O' course I read it!

Obviously a lot of people read it. It even meant enough to some people to put him here in this hospital," Cedric fired back. "But all that talk about cooperative solutions and individual responsibility, that stuff has got to work both ways. Otherwise, that's all it is. It's just talk."

"Well, I'm glad to see you got the message," Pops responded with a disapproving shake of his head.

"All I know is," Cedric retaliated, "if someone hits you with a stick, you've got to find a bigger stick."

"A bigger stick, huh?" Pops repeated with a sarcastic edge in his voice.

"That's right, a bigger stick," Cedric affirmed. "You've got to become the stick-er instead of the stick-ee."

"Oh, that's pretty. You think of that all by yourself, Mr. Poet?"

"It may not be pretty, but writing a letter to their mommies only leaves you with one thing at the end of the day."

"And what's that?" Pops asked.

"Your ass kicked," Cedric responded.

"Now, don't get too brave with me, boy," Pops warned as he moved closer to Cedric, who wasn't backing down. "I am not a man to be bold with right now."

Suddenly the nurse rushed in. "May I ask what is going on in here, please?"

Everybody stopped in their tracks and the room became silent again. Whatever was going on certainly was not about to be explained to the nurse. Cedric lowered his arms in disgust. Shawn grabbed Cedric and, without another word, dragged him out of the room. A moment later, Gwen stormed out and took off in the opposite direction from Shawn and Cedric. She didn't say anything either.

Pops sat back down and put his head in his hands. The nurse looked around again to determine if there was going to be any more trouble, but with Cedric, Shawn, and Gwen gone, she figured the storm had passed and it would be okay to let the rest of the visitors stay. Satisfied that everyone was alerted to behave, the nurse exited.

Mr. Jarvin approached Pops and tenderly put his hand on his shoulder.

"Mr. Anderson. Mrs. Anderson. I would like you to know how truly sorry I am. If I had had any idea that something like this could have happened . . ."

"Don't blame yourself, Mr. Jarvin," Mrs. Anderson said to him. "There was no way you could have been aware that people like this were out there plotting to do something this horrible."

"Well," said Mr. Jarvin, at a loss for words. "Maybe I . . ." and his voice trailed off. The room fell silent except for the hum of medical machines monitoring Andre's vital signs.

"Anyway, on behalf of myself and everyone down at the magazine, I just want you to know that our insurance is going to take care of all the hospital bills and so forth. I know it's not much but, well, we all feel just terrible. Just terrible. Everybody is simply wrecked over what has happened. I mean, it's the least we can do."

Jarvin paused, struggling with his emotions.

"It's, it's just such a tragedy. For something so good to result in something so bad, well, it defies explanation. If God is watching, it just . . . it just makes a man wonder." He rubbed his brow. "Well, like I said, everyone down at the magazine is just devastated. I only wish there was something more I could do."

Jarvin crossed the room and shook Pops's hand and then Mrs. Anderson's. After that he picked up his briefcase and approached the edge of the hospital bed.

"Andre, I . . . I'm sorry," Mr. Jarvin said, lifting his eyes to look at Andre face-to-face. But Andre wouldn't turn his head. He sat there expressionless, as expressionless as he had been all day. "I really hope you feel better soon. If there is anything at all that I can do for you, don't hesitate to ask."

Mr. Jarvin looked at Andre almost as if he were asking for forgiveness. Andre's expression still remained blank and empty. It was as if Jarvin were talking to a wall.

Finally, after getting no response whatsoever, no forgiveness, no acknowledgment, no anything, Jarvin shifted his briefcase from one hand to the other and turned toward the door.

"I'd better be going. See you soon, Andre." He walked quietly out of the hospital room.

Mrs. Anderson moved closer to Pops, put her hand in his, and squeezed it. The room was quiet again.

A tear came to Andre's eye and rolled down his cheek. He didn't even raise his good hand to wipe it away.

XVII

Mrs. Anderson hung up the telephone.

"Is it okay if I use it now?" Theresa asked in her usual self-absorbed manner.

"But if call waiting rings, you click over, you hear?" Mrs. Anderson warned her.

"Yes, Mom," Theresa said, knowing that her actions might not exactly follow her words.

Pops sat in his favorite chair watching television, the volume, as usual, blaring. He eyed his wife with a squinted glare as she crossed in front of him on her way to Andre's room. Though Mr. Anderson and Mrs. Anderson did not say a word out loud at the moment, there was a great deal of communication going on between them. And Pops wasn't happy about any of it.

Andre's door was closed. Mrs. Anderson softly knocked. There was no reply. She knocked again.

"Andre?" Still no response. She opened his door.

Andre lay in bed wearing a plain gray T-shirt. His arm was still bandaged, but not as thickly as it had been. The swelling in his face was practically gone.

"Andre, that was Gwen on the phone," Mrs. Anderson said, poking her head inside the door. "She just wanted to know how you were feeling."

Andre didn't respond.

"Well, I told her that maybe you would call her back a little later, if you felt like it, of course. Also, Shawn, Cedric, people from the magazine, from school—shoot, feels like the whole dang world has been calling," Mrs. Anderson told him. "Honey, if you're up to it, maybe it would make you feel better to call some of them back?"

Andre remained still, seemingly deaf to what his mother was saying.

"Everybody sends their love," she added in an encouraging sort of way.

All Andre could do was stare at the ceiling. There were no words.

"You know, tonight we're having barbecued pork chops for dinner. Your favorite, Andre. It will be ready in about forty-five minutes if you want to join us. If not," Mrs. Anderson said with a pause, "well, I understand. I'll just bring you a plate in here."

Andre continued to stare at the blank space in front of him without responding.

"Just remember, baby. I love you. Lots of people love you."

After another silent, nonresponsive moment, Mrs. Anderson backed out of the room and shut the door behind her.

When the door closed Andre rolled over in his bed and pulled from underneath his covers a copy of *Affairs*. The page was open to the article he had written. For what must have been the fiftieth time that day, Andre began reading it.

Shawn walked out of his house wrestling with a stuffed garbage bag. His mother had made a liquidy lemon-chicken dish, but it hadn't turned out well and Shawn was stuck with the task of transferring the calamity from inside the house to outside the house without any of the toxic juice leaking from the garbage bag onto the carpet. As he approached the curb and dumped the bag into the trash can, a dark blue four-door Lincoln with four black men inside pulled up. All were wearing sunglasses. It was nighttime.

Shawn stopped cold. He didn't know who they were. A jolt of fear raced through his veins. Without warning, the guy in the front seat rolled down the window and stared at Shawn. Then he took off his sunglasses. It was Cedric.

"Hey, Ced," Shawn said, tentatively approaching the car and looking inside. While relieved to see a familiar face, his feelings about the vehicle still hadn't changed. None of the others in the car were familiar to him. "What you fellas up to?" Shawn asked.

"We up to finding some retribution," Cedric responded as he slowly lifted his shirt and flashed a gun.

"Get in," he said to Shawn.

"You found the guys who messed up Andre?" Shawn asked.

"Put it this way," Cedric replied. "We know of some guys who ain't exactly sad about the whole situation, if you know what I mean."

Shawn paused and then looked again at the other guys in the car. They still had not taken off their glasses.

"I don't know, Ced. That ain't the same, man."

"Yo, screw this white boy," one of the guys in the back said with venom in his voice. "We don't need him to go smoke some racists."

"Yeah, it's a black thing anyway. What's his white ass understand?" said another menacing voice from the back.

"Hey, chill out. Shawn ain't like that," Cedric told them and unlocked his door to get out of the car. "I'll be back in a sec."

"Where you goin' C-Man?" asked the driver.

"Yo, I'll be back in a sec."

Cedric led Shawn away from the car for a private talk. "I thought you was down with this," he said.

"Well, I am. I mean, I think I am, but I don't know if I'm down with *this*, you know what I'm saying?"

"Hey, man, we gotta do this. We gotta do this for Andre."

"Dude, you can't just go blastin' people to make up for what happened to Andre. That ain't right."

"What ain't right is what happened to my cousin," Cedric fired back. "I'm doing this for Andre."

"Nah, you ain't doing this for Andre," Shawn responded, shaking his head back and forth. "You're doing this for yourself."

"Oh, what you know?"

"Man, you might wax an innocent person. Then what? Those fools in that car, they don't care. They're just into the shooting and all that mess. But you ain't like them, Ced. You ain't like them at all."

Shawn took a deep breath. Most of those guys in the car probably didn't even know Andre, he thought. But how does a white kid like Shawn say that to a black kid like Cedric, even if they are close friends?

"I thought you was down, but maybe this is a black thing that you can't never understand," Cedric said. "Maybe we ain't as tight as I once thought."

"Yeah, you're right there. I won't never know

what it's like to be a black man in this country," Shawn responded. "But I'll tell you this, I thought about what Pops said and it makes sense. Violence ain't the cure for violence. Peace is. I mean watcha gonna do, take out a white boy just to send a message?"

"Naw, we gonna take out two. We Fed Ex–ing this telegram."

Shawn shook his head again.

"You ain't like that, Ced. You ain't like that at all."

Cedric paused and thought about it. The driver climbed out of the car and glared at them.

"Yo, C-Man, let's go."

"I mean, damn, we got to roll, brother," came that menacing voice from the backseat again.

Cedric turned to Shawn. "I got to do something."

"Not this, Ced," Shawn said, backing away. "Not this."

"Yo, C-Man!" the driver shouted. "Let's roll, homie."

Cedric looked at the car, looked at Shawn, and then looked back at the car again.

"You ain't coming?" he asked.

Shawn shook his head. "Naw, I ain't coming."

Cedric walked back over to the car and opened the door.

"Think about it, Ced. You're smarter than this, dude," Shawn told him as he climbed in the car.

Cedric put his sunglasses back on. "Maybe I am. Maybe I'm not."

Cedric closed the car door and the vehicle rolled away.

XVIII

Roast beef, mashed potatoes, homemade biscuits, green beans, butter, soda, milk, water, root beer, salad, salt and pepper were spread out over the dining room table from end to end. Pops, Theresa, Tina, Teddy, and Mrs. Anderson were seated in front of the steaming plates, about to start dinner. One chair was glaringly empty.

"Pass me a root beer," Teddy commanded Tina.

"Say the magic word," Tina said.

"Pass me a root beer, knucklehead," Teddy replied.

"Ma-awm, Teddy called me a knucklehead."

"Teddy, don't call your sister names, and have a glass of milk. I don't want you drinking so much soda," Mrs. Anderson said as she made sure everybody's plate had a bit of what she wanted them to have on it. Theresa got vegetables, Tina got a well-done piece of meat, and Pops had the salt taken away from his side of the table because his hypertension was starting to become a problem again.

Tina, being the baby of the family, nibbled on a biscuit and waited for Theresa, who was taking her sweet time, to cut her food.

"Is Andre going to eat with us tonight, Mommy?" Tina asked. A hush fell over the table.

"Um, I don't think so, dear," her mother answered. "Andre still isn't feeling very well."

"Been over three weeks since the boy's been home and he still ain't said a damn word," Pops mumbled to no one in particular.

"Now, you just stop right there," Mrs. Anderson ordered from across the table. "We're having a nice supper tonight. I don't want to hear another word about it."

"Mommy, did those bad men who smushed Andre's hand smush out his tongue too?" Tina asked.

Pops glared at his wife.

"No, dear," Mrs. Anderson replied in a calm voice. "Andre's tongue is fine. It's just that, well, Andre is still in a great deal of pain. The shock of what has happened to him hasn't fully left him yet."

"Will he ever talk again, Mommy?" Teddy asked, not fully understanding either.

"Of course he will, sweetheart. Of course he will. Now, let me see you eat some vegetables and—" Mrs. Anderson stopped in midsentence.

Andre was standing in the doorway.

The entire family turned to look. They stared at him for a moment. No one was sure how long he had been there.

Mrs. Anderson finally broke the stilted silence by clanking a serving spoon against the inside of the bowl of green beans and putting a nice big scoop on Teddy's plate. Slowly there were more clanks of silverware as everybody went back to eating dinner.

Andre quietly took his regular seat. Mrs. Anderson began piling food on his plate. Although she served him with a calm expression, as if it were just another dish of food she was making up on just another Sunday night, she felt her blood pumping and her heart racing. It was amazing that she didn't spill Andre's dinner all over Tina's head.

Mrs. Anderson loaded a tasty-looking lump of mashed potatoes onto Andre's plate. "Would you like a bit more than that, dear?" she asked Andre.

He waved his hand over his plate and shook his head no. Pops watched with an unhappy glare as Mrs. Anderson set down Andre's food in front of him. Andre reached for the pepper.

"Your mother asked if you would like any more mashed potatoes, Andre," Pops said from his chair at the head of the table.

Andre raised his eyes to look at his father.

Pops set down the forkful of food he was about to place in his mouth. "You know, you could say, 'No, thank you, Mom, I don't want any more mashed potatoes.'"

Mrs. Anderson nervously picked up the plate of roast beef.

"He said he didn't want any more," she said to her husband, then changed the subject. "Now, how about another piece of roast beef, dear? Look, I have an end cut. You love end cuts."

"I don't want no end cut!" Pops snapped back. He stared at Andre. "Do you want some more mashed potatoes, Andre?"

Everybody stopped. The table grew uncomfortably quiet.

Pops waited for an answer. Andre lowered his eyes and didn't say a word. Theresa, Teddy, and Tina sat frozen in their chairs. Nobody dared move.

"I asked if you would like some more mashed potatoes, Andre?" Pops repeated.

The table remained as still as a cemetery. Andre slowly raised his eyes to look at his father. Pops glowered back at him. Andre opened his mouth as if he just might say something. Pops waited. Another moment passed.

"'Yes, I would love some mashed potatoes, Mother! Thank you!'" Pops yelled out. "'No, I'm set, Mom! No more mashed potatoes for me!'" Pops's voice grew even louder. "'Well, on second thought, maybe just a tad bit more of mashed potatoes would be great!'" *Bam!* Pops slammed his fist down, rattling every dish, spoon, and fork on the table. The children jumped. "'No way! No more mashed potatoes for me. I am stuffed!'" Pops shouted as he stood up from his chair. "'Mashed potatoes? Hell, yes, I would love some more mashed potatoes. Load 'em on up there, Mom. I'm a growing boy!'"

The children were terrified.

"'Would somebody please pass me the mashed potatoes? I want some more *goddamn mashed pota-toes*!'"

Suddenly, Andre rose from his chair and dashed out of the room. Pops threw down his napkin into his uneaten food.

"Andre!" Mrs. Anderson called out. But it was too late. The front door had already slammed shut.

Mrs. Anderson stared at her husband, who was fuming mad. The whole family sat in silence as dinner grew cold. Everyone's appetite was just like Andre . . . gone.

XIX

The night was clear and crisp. Andre, deep in thought, walked across the deserted basketball court, silhouetted by the light of the three-quarter moon. He gazed at the basket. The net waved slightly in the breeze.

Andre meandered over to the foul line and set himself up to take a pretend foul shot. He bent at the knees, arched his back, and imitated dribbling the ball once before putting up a shot.

Andre raised his hands to shoot—and then stopped. The sight of his right hand all wrapped in bandages made him pause. He looked again at the rim and then back at his hand and then straightened his knees and stopped pretending. He didn't take a shot.

A noise could be heard in the distance. It was the faint crunch of footsteps now growing louder and louder. Andre didn't bother to turn around to see who it was. What difference does it make, he thought.

The footsteps stopped.

"Yeah, you were fouled," a voice said. It was Shawn. He was holding a box. Andre continued to stare at the basketball rim without turning around.

"Your mother called. I thought I might find you here. She's really concerned."

Andre didn't respond.

"We all are, ya know?"

Andre still didn't say a word. Shawn shifted his feet and kind of kicked the ground, looking down.

"I, I just don't know what to say, Andre. I mean I love you, man. I really love you like, like you were my brother. I just don't know what I can do."

Emotion built up in Andre's face, but he still didn't, or couldn't, spin around to face Shawn.

"Well," Shawn continued. "I made you a gift."

Shawn set the box down at Andre's feet.

"It's the only thing I could think of." Shawn paused. "If there is anything I can do, you know, just ask."

Shawn put his hands in his pockets and, not knowing what to do, slowly turned to walk away.

Andre stood at the foul line with the box at his feet. After a moment he bent over and picked it up.

It was difficult for Andre to open the box. Shawn, who had stopped and was now watching, was in no way going to walk back over and help Andre as he struggled. He would have to figure out a way to open it himself. Andre tugged at the top with minor success. Shawn waited patiently.

Finally, Andre was able to open the box. He reached inside and slowly pulled out a wrapped something or other. With his teeth Andre pulled the tissue paper off the object to reveal what it was.

Andre held it up in wonder. It was a hand. A beautiful lifelike sculpture of a right hand. The moonlight made it glisten.

A tear rolled down Andre's cheek. And then another and another. Then, unable to restrain his emotions any longer, Andre started to weep.

"I'm just so empty," he said through heaving sobs. "So empty."

Shawn ran back over and gave him a hug. A big, bearlike hug.

"It's all right, man. Let it go. Let it go, Andre."

Andre began crying harder and harder, weeping like a child. Shawn hugged him with all the love he had as Andre released his pain and grief.

After another moment or two of sobbing, Andre gathered a bit of composure and took a half step back.

"Do you know what the craziest part is?" Andre asked. He began laughing through his tears.

"The craziest part about the whole thing is that I'm left-handed. Those idiots butchered the wrong hand." Andre let out a burst of laughter that combined with a wail of suffering and shook his whole body from head to toe.

Wiping the tears that ran down his face on the sleeve of his Hoopster sweatshirt, Andre shook his head and chuckled even more at the ridiculousness of the whole thing.

"It's gonna be all right, buddy," Shawn said with another hug. "It's gonna be all right."

Another quiet moment passed. Andre's sobbing began to slow.

"Oh, man," Shawn said with a deep exhalation, thankful that his friend was back from whatever dark place he had been. "What the heck are we gonna do?"

Andre wiped more tears from his eyes.

"I don't know," he responded and then looked Shawn directly in the eye. "But I do know that I will type with my goddamned nose if I have to."

With a smile on his face, Shawn gave Andre another huge hug. This time Andre hugged back.

After they separated, Andre noticed that Shawn had a tear in his eye. "Damn dust," Shawn said as he rubbed his eye. "You think they'd clean up out here or something."

"Yeah, it is pretty dusty tonight," Andre answered, looking up into the clear night sky.

"Say," Andre asked after thinking about it for a second. "How'd you get down here anyway? I know you didn't walk."

"Your dad gave me a ride."

Andre quickly turned and saw the taillights of a vehicle in the distance exit the parking lot.

"You ready to go back?" Shawn asked.

"Yeah, I think so."

"Good, then hustle up, dude. I want to get to your house before your mom puts away the roast beef."

Andre laughed. It was the first time, well, the second time, in a long, long while.

Shawn picked up the box for Andre and they walked off the basketball court. The nets swayed gently in the breeze behind them.

XX

The *beep! beep!* of a car horn from out in front of the house could be heard inside.

"Come on, Andre. We don't want to be late," Mrs. Anderson called out as she deftly stuck into her earlobe a gold earring that perfectly complemented her striking red dress. "Let's go."

Andre popped out of his room, smoothing out the sleeves of a crisp black tuxedo. While his right hand was still wrapped in a cast, it was just a small one, covering only his hand. He looked sharp.

"All right. All right, I'm coming," Andre said as he glided into the living room. Tuxedoes were the perfect attire in which to glide.

"Wow! You look great, Andre," Mrs. Anderson said when she saw her son.

"*¡Qué caliente!*" Gwen remarked as she stepped up and gave Andre a kiss. She knew a big smooch would ruin her lipstick, but she didn't care. "You look terrific," she whispered in Andre's ear.

"And I must say, you ladies look absolutely

fantastic," Andre noted, a compliment that made both his girlfriend and his mother feel beautiful. Andre had always had the gift of making others feel good about themselves.

Shawn and Cedric, dressed handsomely in coats and ties themselves, coughed to get Andre's attention.

"Eh-ehem!" the two said at the same time.

"Oh, but of course," Andre answered with a big show of appreciation. "You gentlemen look magnificent as well."

Cedric and Shawn straightened their ties, hamming it up all the way.

Andre crossed the room and gave each of them the trademark up-over-and-around high five. They pulled at Andre's bow tie playfully.

"I would say the gentleman has come a long way," Cedric said with a British accent.

"Indeed he has. Indeed he has," Shawn answered, following Cedric's lead.

Another *beep! beep! beep!* came from out front. The beeps were getting longer.

"Let's go in there!" Pops yelled from outside. "We don't want to be late."

Mrs. Anderson approached Andre and brushed some imaginary lint off his jacket. A tear started to form in her eye.

"My boy, the honored guest at the International Magazine Association's annual banquet. I am so proud."

"Thanks, Mom," Andre said. "But, please, try not to cry."

"Okay," she said, but it was too late. She was already crying.

"I love you, Mom," Andre said.

Mrs. Anderson gave Andre a big, smothering hug. "I love you, too, baby."

She and Andre stood in the center of the room, hugging, when all of a sudden the door was thrown wide open.

"What is the matter with you, woman?" Pops shouted out as he burst inside. He wore a sleek black dinner jacket with a blazing purple shirt that might blind anyone who stared at it for too long. "The boy is gonna be late. You want him to be late? I don't want him to be late. Shawn, do you want him to be late?"

"No, I don't want him to be late," replied Shawn.

"Gwen, do you want him to be late?" Pops asked again.

"No, I don't want him to be late," she answered with a nervous shake of her head.

"Cedric, do you want him to be late?" Pops asked with a turn of his head.

"Well, if circumstances happen to dictate that lateness is going to be an occurrence then—"

"Just hush up, birdbrain. I got no time for your foolishness," Pops said, shaking his head. "Now, we gotta go. And I don't mean in ten minutes. I mean now."

"Don't worry, Pops. If they have to, they can wait," Andre said, trying to calm his father down.

"The show don't start at eight," Pops barked back. "The show starts at seven-thirty. Imagine that. The guest of honor doesn't even know what time the biggest speech of his life begins." Pops turned and headed for the door, mumbling to himself on the way out to the car, baffled by their dillydallying.

"I just can't figure it," he said to himself as he shook his head. "The boy should know what time the program starts. I mean, he's supposed to be intelligent. It just don't make sense."

Everyone smiled.

"Don't mind him none, we have plenty of time," Mrs. Anderson said. "It's just 'cause he's so proud of you that he's nervous."

"I thought he was nervous because he was getting ready to start college this week," Cedric chimed in.

"Now, Cedric, don't you tease him about that. You know he's sensitive," Mrs. Anderson warned.

"Imagine that, a fifty-three-year-old freshman. Tell me again, how many times do you have to have flunk kindergarten to move through our educational system at that kind of pace?"

"Cedric . . ." Mrs. Anderson warned.

"All right, all right, I'll leave him alone . . . tonight," Cedric promised. "But when classes start, you can bet your behind he is not going to be watching any TV until he has finished all his homework."

Mrs. Anderson rolled her eyes. She knew Pops was going to be in for it.

Andre looked around the house and took a deep breath. He knew he was no longer the same person he once had been.

"Well, should we go?" Gwen asked.

"Yeah," Andre responded with a sigh that indicated he was as ready as he would ever be.

Shawn held the front door open. "After you, ladies."

"Thank you," Gwen and Mrs. Anderson said as they filed, arm in arm, out of the house to get the whole group into the cars.

When Cedric got to the front door Shawn cut him off and beat him out the door. "I know when I said *ladies* you got a bit confused, but . . ." Shawn dashed out the door with a laugh.

"Oh yeah?" Cedric said as he made a move to rush outside and get his two cents in, but suddenly Andre grabbed Cedric by the elbow and pulled him back inside for a quick moment of privacy.

"Yo, Ced, wait a sec," Andre said.

"Yeah sure, Andre. You okay?" Cedric asked, concerned.

"Me? Yeah, I'm cool," Andre responded. "I just wanted to, you know, say thanks. Thanks for what you did."

Cedric paused, reflecting on what Andre was trying to tell him. "But I didn't do anything," he answered, a bit ashamed.

"Yeah, I know," Andre responded, proud of his cousin. "That is what I'm talking about."

Cedric looked up. He hadn't done anything that night in the dark blue four-door Lincoln. He hadn't done anything any other night either. And though he had wanted to many other times, nights and days, he hadn't.

And he was still never sure if he had made the right choice.

A smile came to Cedric's face. "You the man, Andre. You the man," he said as he threw his arm around his cousin's shoulder and the two of them exited the house.

The entire crew packed into car, three in the front, three in the back, buzzing with excitement. Cedric's mouth ran nonstop and Pops, despite protesting that he wanted Cedric to shut up, was just as entertained by Cedric's infinite ability to comment upon everyone and everything as were all the other people in the car.

"Ya ever notice how motorcycle cops always have a mustache? Does it really help keep their face that much warmer? And how come when some drunk is driving a hundred and seventy-five miles per hour in a school zone they are nowhere to be found, but let a person jaywalk in a grocery-store parking lot and all of a sudden the SWAT team appears with Uzis a-blazin'?"

Andre sat next to the window in the backseat. Nobody minded that he wasn't talkative. He seemed to prefer just looking out at the scenery. He'd seen streets like these a thousand times before, yet this time they seemed new and different.

The car approached a red light and stopped. Across the way there was a basketball court. Some guys, unfamiliar to Andre, were playing a game of pickup hoop, Shirts versus Skins.

Andre, dressed in his tuxedo, stared out the car window at the action on the court. One of the players faked left, pulled up for a jump shot, and drained it from long distance. His teammates smiled and gave him high fives as they ran back down the other way to play some D.

Andre looked down at his hand and felt the texture of the cast. He tried to squeeze his fingers and make a fist, but his hand was just not strong enough.

The traffic light turned green and the car started to pull away. Everybody, especially Cedric, was still yapping excitedly. Andre touched his hand affectionately, took a deep breath, and tuned back into the conversation.

XXI

In the large and elegant Downtown Banquet Hall a crowd of well-dressed people sat and chatted at tables that were done up for the big reception. A stage and podium were at the front of the room, indicating the place from which Andre would be speaking. Cedric and Shawn knew they were in for something special when they saw that each place setting had three plates, two knives, three forks, three spoons, and two glasses.

"Wow, fancy. Check out this teeny-tiny fork. What do you think we're gonna eat with this?" Shawn asked.

"Who cares about the damn fork; where's our waiter? I need me some vino," Cedric said, reaching for a glass.

Mr. Jarvin approached the microphone and the audience began to settle down.

"Tonight's guest speaker," Mr. Jarvin began, looking quite sharp in a tux himself, "is a young man with, well, how can I say this? He is a young man with great courage. Originally I had the pleasure of meeting Andre Anderson. . . ."

Backstage Andre waited in the wings while Mr. Jarvin introduced him. Behind Andre stood a stagehand, a white guy, about twenty-five years old. He had long hair and a few tattoos, and was dressed in a heavy-metal T-shirt and blue jeans. The stagehand pushed a button here, turned a knob there, and generally monitored things at the lighting control console while Andre waited for his cue to go on.

Suddenly, Andre had an itch under his cast. Although he tried to scratch it, he couldn't get to it. He turned his arm upside down, twisted it left, then right, but still, no matter what he did, he just couldn't get to the right spot. The stagehand, noticing Andre's dilemma, reached into his tool kit and pulled out a long, thin strand of copper wire.

"Here, try this," the stagehand said as he offered the strand to Andre.

Andre looked at the wire, then at the stagehand. "Thanks," he said, taking the strand. "I guess my hands are sweating a bit. It's warm in this suit."

"Yeah, it does get hot in a suit," the stagehand responded knowingly, although he didn't have the look of a man who wore a tuxedo too often. "But I wouldn't be nervous if I were you," he added. "See, my philosophy for getting up in front of crowds is just to pretend that everyone is in their underwear. It's a good philosophy. Works great every time for nerves."

"My grandmother's out there," Andre pointed out.

"Ooh, that might backfire then," the stagehand replied, now at a loss for further advice. He turned back to his console.

"I'm not really that nervous, though," Andre confessed. "I thought I was going to be, but I'm really not."

The stagehand did a double take and turned around again. "Hey, I know you," he said. "Ain't you that guy who wrote that thing and then got beat up bad by those racists?"

Andre looked at his shoes. "Yeah, I'm the guy."

"Man, that was pretty heavy. Did they ever catch those dudes?"

Andre paused and gazed out onstage. Mr. Jarvin was still speaking.

"No."

"Well, that sucks. I mean, what happened to you was crap, man. Just plain evil," he said. "But I wouldn't worry about it if I were you, 'cause everybody gets theirs in the end, you know? Everybody. You dig what I'm saying?"

"Yeah," Andre said, looking away. Andre hoped

the stagehand would get the hint that he really didn't want to continue with this conversation anymore. After all, in about three minutes' time, Andre had to go out and give a major speech to a crowded banquet hall. He would have thought the stagehand would have respected that.

He didn't.

"I mean, that's my philosophy, man," the stagehand continued, as if he and Andre were now good pals. "Believe me, I know about philosophy, 'cause I used to steal stuff. You know, like candy bars and disposable lighters and hi-fi stereo equipment. Then one day it happened. *Bam!*" The stagehand slammed his fist on the console so hard that Andre jumped. "It just happened."

"What happened?" Andre asked, his curiosity getting the better of him.

This slight bit of interest seemed to be just what the stagehand was looking for and he turned completely away from his knobs and dials. "See, one day I borrowed my mother's car without asking her and I went to the record store and bought, like, seven or eight totally hot CDs. I'm talking total jammers. Not any of that hip-hop, rap-music crap. Real music." The stagehand didn't stop to consider that maybe Andre liked hip-hop and rap, which he certainly did. "Then

I went to a movie with a buddy of mine," he continued. "And when I came out, the car was stolen. I mean, the whole damn car, my new CDs, and everything. That's when I knew, man. I just knew."

"Knew what?" Andre asked.

"Knew about the need for a good philosophy, man. I mean, everybody has got to have a good philosophy. Otherwise, you're cooked."

"Cooked?"

"Cooked," the stagehand responded, very sure of himself.

"Yeah," Andre replied as he turned to hear Mr. Jarvin's final remarks. "I guess."

"No, really, man, it is. A good philosophy is everything. It makes for a good life."

Andre turned around and mulled these last few words over.

"What was that?" Andre asked.

"A good philosophy makes for a good life," the stagehand repeated. "Everybody has got to have one."

"You learn that in school?" Andre asked.

"School? No way, man. I hate homework."

"Church?"

The stagehand laughed. "Yeah, right."

"No, seriously, where'd you learn that?" Andre asked, now genuinely interested.

The stagehand paused and then looked Andre dead in the eye. "Man, I learned that in life."

The stagehand turned back to fuss with the console. Andre spent a moment digesting his words.

"Now, remember, don't be nervous out there. Just go get 'em."

"I told you, I'm not nervous."

"You're not? I would be," the stagehand responded. "There must be more than five hundred people in the audience."

"But you just said that . . ."

"I know what I just said, but I only did that to make you feel better. You kiddin'? I'd be nervous as hell if I had to go out there," the stagehand said as he peeped around the curtain and looked over the audience. "Looks like it could be a pretty tough crowd, too."

"Thanks," Andre replied with a small shake of his head.

"So?" said the stagehand.

"So what?" replied Andre.

"So how come you ain't nervous?"

Andre checked over his tux and straightened his posture. "I don't know. Maybe it's because I have something to say."

The stagehand nodded his head in approval.

Andre offered him back his strand of copper wire.

"Naw, keep it, man," the stagehand said. "We're all in this together."

"Thanks," Andre replied, sticking it into his inside pocket.

"And now, it is my great pleasure to introduce to you Mr. Andre Anderson," Mr. Jarvin announced.

The crowd began to applaud as Andre took the stage. At first, only his family and friends rose to their feet—his grandparents, his uncles, a couple of heavy-set aunts—but within a few moments the whole audience was out of their chairs, cheering wildly. Mr. Jarvin welcomed Andre to the podium with a hug and whispered "Congratulations" in his ear before exiting the stage. Andre waited a minute so everyone could be seated again and settle down.

Looking out into a sea of faces, some of them familiar, most of them not, Andre reflected on the scene and noticed something. All of the audience members seemed to share one thing in common. They were all smiling.

"Ladies and gentlemen, thank you for having me here tonight," Andre began. "I appreciate this honor deeply."

A few water glasses softly clinked in the back of the room. "Many people have asked me about justice.

As most of you know, my attackers were never caught. Am I angry about that? Yeah, I'm not going to lie to you. I was incredibly angry. I—"

Andre suddenly stopped, pausing a moment to collect himself. It wasn't thirty seconds into his speech and he was already getting so choked up, he wasn't sure if he would be able to continue. The audience waited.

"You know," Andre continued as he regained some of his composure, "for months, all I wanted was payback. People had hurt me. I wanted to hurt them back."

Faces in the crowd nodded in understanding.

"Hurt them bad."

Andre stopped again and looked down at his hand. He squeezed his fingers, but his grip wasn't the same as it used to be. It would never be the same.

"And at the moment my hate was greatest, when my blood was boiling, when the images raging through my mind were nothing other than vengeance, violence, and retribution, I came to understand one thing. . . ."

Andre gazed into the distance. The room was silent.

"I came to understand that there is no such thing as revenge."

Andre dropped his head almost as if he were ashamed of his realization. It was like he felt there should have been something more. Something more electric. Something more fulfilling. Something more spectacular and noble and dangerous and blood-stirring. But there wasn't.

Andre simply understood that there was just no such thing as revenge. The past was over and the future was his—and his alone—to create.

"I mean, maybe I could hurt the people who hurt me—if I could even find them—but what would I get from that? Would I feel better?" Andre shook his head. "Naw, I'm the kind of person who would feel worse. Doin' wrong like that could never make me feel right."

Andre looked down from the stage and made eye contact with a man sitting in the front row of the audience.

"I just thank God I didn't throw my life away trying to pursue it."

The entire room followed Andre's gaze and looked over at the middle-aged man dressed in purple in the front row. Pops tried to ignore the attention, but he felt the stares of the crowd like a wave of heat. Pops tried to ignore the tear rolling down his face, but he felt the itch on his cheek like the small tickle of a feather. The only thing Pops didn't try to ignore was the pride in his heart he felt for his son. And he didn't give a damn who knew 'bout it, either.

"Thank you, Pops," Andre said from the stage.

A small smattering of claps grew into a round of applause from the audience. Pops thought the crowd was clapping for his son. Andre thought the crowd was clapping for his father. They were both right.

"So," Andre asked as he turned back toward the audience, "will justice be served? I think so. People can run from the police, but they can't run from what they deserve."

Another round of applause arose from the audience.

"And I may be naive, but I still believe in doing the right thing. And I still believe in speaking up when something is wrong. And I still believe in taking individual responsibility for our actions. But most important," Andre boomed as he took command of the podium. "Most important, I still believe in me. And they can't ever take that."

The crowd rose from their chairs like a swell on the sea and erupted into an ovation. People stood from their seats and clapped so hard their hands turned red. Gwen passed Mrs. Anderson a tissue to wipe her tears, but Pops, now a leaky faucet from both of his own eyes, intercepted it for himself.

Yet, out of all the people in the room, no one was more proud than Theresa.

Andre exited the stage. He may have walked on like a victim, but he walked off like a champion.

"Nicely done, dude," Andre heard a voice say. "That's a good philosophy."

"Thanks, man, I'm glad you think so," replied Andre. "'Cause a good philosophy makes for a good life." Andre paused. He and the stagehand exchanged a knowing smile . . . then a high five.

"You all right, dude. You all right."

"So are you."

The rest of the night was nothing more than a fantastical blur.

XXII

*S*WISH! A shot rang through the hoop.

Cedric dribbled the basketball up-court going the other way, his tongue waggling in the wind as he talked smack to the defender who was guarding him.

"Now I am going to show you the move that made Michael Jordan retire for the thirty-second time."

Cedric juked to the left, faked right, penetrated the lane, and tried a one-handed, double-pump, reverse layup off the glass. It didn't come anywhere close to going in.

"Foul!" Cedric cried. "I was fouled."

"Man, I didn't touch you," Petey yelled back.

"You did so. You got me right here," Cedric explained as he pointed to his arm. "You got me right here on the inside of my forearm where the bilateral tendon meets the optomical ventrical joint."

"What the heck is an optomical ventrical joint?" Petey asked.

"You see. You done fouled me in a place you

didn't even know existed. Gimme the ball," Cedric ordered.

"I didn't see no foul," said a voice off to the side of the court.

Everybody turned and froze in their tracks. It was Andre. Aside from a small bandage on his right hand, Andre was dressed in shorts, high-tops and a T-shirt that said THE HOOPSTER across the front of it.

The quiet held for a moment.

"Well, can I get a game, or what?" Andre asked.

Suddenly, everybody ran over and welcomed Andre back with smiles and high fives.

"What's up, Andre?"

"Yo, good to see ya."

"How's the hand, man?"

"We'll see, we'll see," Andre said. "Been doing lots of rehab so, well, we'll see."

Cedric tossed Andre the ball. He held it for a minute in his hands. The orange skin felt like an old friend.

Andre took a dribble—once with his left hand . . . then again . . . then he bounced it over to his right hand and back again to his left. Slowly he picked up the pace. Faster, faster. He went left, right, left, crossed it over once, dribbled back to front between his legs and then back again. He didn't appear to have lost a step.

Andre casually walked up to the basket to take a lazy shot, a nice, easy layup right under the rim just to get his feel back. He lifted the ball, tossed it up, and—*bam!* A hand came swooping across the sky and swatted Andre's shot clear back to yesteryear.

Rejected!

Andre turned around to see who had done it. It was Shawn.

"No, no, no, no, no!" Shawn said, waving his finger back and forth at Andre. "None of that easy stuff out here. You want a bucket, you gotta earn a bucket."

Shawn retrieved the basketball and then tossed a hard pass at Andre's chest. Andre caught it and looked up.

He paused. "Oh, is that so?" Andre asked.

"Always has been, always will be," Shawn replied. Shawn was very sweaty and very serious.

"Come on, Shawn, give my boy a break," Cedric said, walking over and stepping between them. "It's his first day back."

"Bring it on."

"I'm sorry," Shawn responded. "Were you talking to me?"

"That's right," Andre said in a quiet yet firm tone

as he dribbled the ball. "I said, Bring it on. Let's see if you still got it."

"If I still got it? Baby, let's see if *you* still got it," Shawn said as he wiped the sweat from his forehead and crouched down to play a little defense.

"All right then, let's see," Andre replied. Cedric tossed his hands in the air and cleared some space. It was time for a little one-on-one.

Andre started to dribble. Shawn gave him a stiff, hard hand-check in the back and went for the steal. Andre shielded off Shawn with his body and barely retained possession. It was clear that Shawn was not fooling around.

Shawn flashed Andre a cocky smile and tried for the ball again. This time Andre did a better job of protecting it.

Shawn got right up on Andre, playing an in-your-face type of defense. Andre, instead of backing down, went on the offensive and attacked the pressure.

Andre faked to the left, juked right, and changed directions at the top of the key. After leaning in, Andre took a quick step outside the three-point arc and pulled up to gun a long-range shot.

Shawn leaped to block it.

Andre released the ball, sending it flying just

over Shawn's outstretched fingertips. The basketball arched slowly and beautifully through the air. . . .

It didn't need to go in. It didn't have to go in. Andre's life would still have been fine whether it was an airball or not.

But it did go in. . . .

SWISH! Nothing but net.

The whole court fell silent. Shawn gazed at Andre with the dispirited look of a man who has just been torched. After a moment Andre smiled. Then Shawn smiled, too.

"Was there ever a doubt?"